WHATEVER'S BEEN GOING
ON AT MUMBLESBY?

By Colin Watson

Whatever's Been Going On at Mumblesby?

COLIN WATSON

PUBLISHED FOR THE CRIME CLUB BY
DOUBLEDAY & COMPANY, INC.
GARDEN CITY, NEW YORK
1983

All of the characters in this book
are fictitious, and any resemblance
to actual persons, living or dead,
is purely coincidental.

Library of Congress Cataloging in Publication Data

Watson, Colin.
Whatever's been going on at Mumblesby?

I. Title.
PR6073.A86W5   1983   823'914
ISBN 0-385-18382-8
Library of Congress Catalog Card Number 82-45550

WHATEVER'S BEEN GOING ON AT MUMBLESBY?

CHAPTER 1

One of Flaxborough's best-known and respected senior citizens passed away peacefully this week in the person of Mr. Richard Daspard Loughbury. His death took place on Monday at Flaxborough General Hospital after a short illness at Mr. Loughbury's country home, the Manor House, Mumblesby.

"Christ! Guess who's kicked the bucket."

Mr. Loughbury, for many years a solicitor in regular practice in the town, was a noted bowls votary, a Freemason, and at one time a member of Flaxborough Town Council, to whose deliberations he brought wisdom and legal acumen, not unmixed with that brand of humour for which he will be long remembered by local cognoscentes *of the* bon mot. *He was predeceased by his wife five years ago.*

"I said, Guess who's kicked the bucket."

Thus Mr. Brian Lewcock, auctioneer's clerk and not much respected junior citizen, addressed from behind Flaxborough's weekly newspaper the wife who, despite his occasional urging of her to that course, showed no inclination to predecease him.

"All right. Who, then?" Sandra Lewcock came to the end of a row of breakfast-time knitting and with the disengaged needle leaned down to scratch her foot.

"Old Loughbury. Rich Dick."

"Oh, him." Sandra looked down between her knees to see where her ball of wool had gone. She gave the yarn a tug and the ball came running from under the small sideboard like an errant animal. She halted it with a stockinged foot. As she brought the needles into their duel again, she frowned. "Is that right? *Was* he rich? Really rich, I mean?" Her tone suggested doubt, not interest. Sandra's was a thin voice with a petulant lilt.

"He was bloody loaded," said Mr. Lewcock.

Sandra gazed up at the window without slackening the pace of the knitting. "How do you know?"

"Well . . . he was. He must have been. You should see some of the stuff he bought."

"Stuff?"

"At the auctions. Very pricey."

Sandra's scowl deepened. "Auctions? I never saw Mr. Loughbury at an auction."

"No, well you wouldn't, would you," said Mr. Lewcock, his teeth clenched and making him sound like a not very good ventriloquist.

"It was you that said he went to auctions. I don't know what you're on about."

"I never said he went. I said he bought. There is a difference. I'd have thought so, anyway."

"Difference? What do you mean, difference?"

The Flaxborough *Citizen* was slowly lowered in order to give Sandra the full benefit of her husband's long sigh of exasperation. "Mr. Loughbury," he said, with so much ironic emphasis that his voice tripped into falsetto, "never *went* to a sale. He knew what was coming *up*. He had bids put *in* for him. On his *behalf*. By other *people*. Right?"

And he looked fixedly at her thighs. This always made her nervous.

"Who by, for instance?"

"The old man, sometimes." Lewcock meant the head of the firm of auctioneers for which he worked, old Mr. "Noddy" Durham. "Mostly he sent Clapper, though."

"Clapper?"

"Clapper Buxton. His clerk."

Sandra seemed to be thinking. "Did you ever do it?"

"Do what?"

"Bid for him. For Mr. Loughbury."

"I might have."

"You never said."

"So?" Lewcock put more contempt into his stare. Sandra felt her thighs ballooning with unwanted fat.

He looked away at last. He said, "My God!" softly and went back behind the Flaxborough *Citizen* to suck his teeth.

Mr. Loughbury was a lifelong member of the Church of England, and a moving spirit in the Liberal persuasion until he transferred allegiance to the Conservative cause in 1957. He was elected to the chairmanship of the Flaxborough and District Unionist Association in 1970, an office which he held with distinction until illness compelled his recent resignation. Rose growing was his favourite hobby. During the last war Mr. Loughbury achieved the rank of captain in the Boys' Training Corps and also served as a special constable.

"How delightfully inconsequential are our writers of obituaries," remarked Miss Lucilla Edith Cavell Teatime, proprietress of The House of Yesteryear in Northgate. "It would come as no surprise in the midst of so many verbal violets to be told that the late Mr. Loughbury was a keen amateur housebreaker."

Her companion smiled. He was a man rather younger than she, a man with a full, well-nourished face, tending to beard shadow around the chops but otherwise meticulously groomed. His voice, though kindly, possessed that curious timbre conferred by privileged education which puts the less privileged in mind of plums. "I trust you are jesting, Lucy," said this man.

"Of course I am, Edgar." Miss Teatime sighed, and reached towards a small black packet on a shelf of the Welsh dresser beside her chair. "Unfortunately."

Edgar—his name was Harrington, and to favoured clients Miss Teatime confided that his mother had been a lady-in-waiting at Windsor—left his seat at once and handed down the packet and a booklet of matches that lay beside it. He was a compact, but not small, man, probably in his early forties. His bearing and easy movements suggested fitness of an unaggressive kind, derived more likely (thought Miss Teatime) from a regimen of vicarage tennis and spare-time archaeology than from press-ups and squash.

Mr. Harrington was the manager of Miss Teatime's subsidiary enterprise, Gallery Ganby, in the village of Mumblesby, whither he had been drawn some six months previously, partly in response to the invitation of an old friend, but chiefly by reason of his own immediate desire to leave London.

"It would be pleasant upon this summer's day," said Miss Teatime, taking a small cigar from the packet that Edgar had placed by her coffee cup, "to shut up shop and to pay our respects at the house of mourning."

"Is there a widow?"

"None is mentioned."

"Then to whom can we pay our respects?"

Miss Teatime lit her cigar, then blew out the match as if disposing of the question. "There is always someone to receive condolences in the households of the well heeled. It is part of the tidiness that wealth seems to induce."

An "old boy" of Flaxborough Grammar School, Mr. Loughbury pursued his education in Dublin, to which the family moved upon his father's taking up a medical appointment in that city, and later attended Oxford University to study law. He was regarded as an expert

on antiques, of which he built up a notable collection.
A multitude of other interests included study of the his-
tory of fireworks and, in the practical field, work for the
Distressed Ladies Relief Association.

"Would you have said that Richard Loughbury was
an expert on antiques, Mr. Purbright?"

The Chief Constable of Flaxborough, Mr. Harcourt
Chubb, spoke over his shoulder without looking round
at his detective inspector. Mr. Chubb commonly read
the paper while standing, supported lightly against the
fireplace and facing away from the main area of the
office, as if to emphasise the triviality of such an occupation in the context of chief constabledom.

"He certainly seems to have been an expert on their
acquisition, sir. We have his house on the special list."

"I remember Mrs. Chubb asking him to value something that had been in her family for quite a while; it
was a snake—cobra, something of that kind—stuffed, of
course—on a stand—and it had pegs fixed in it to hold
ladies' gloves. He didn't strike me as being particularly
knowledgeable."

There was silence while the chief constable read to
the end of the piece. Then, still without turning round,
he raised his eyes from the paper and spoke with
studied indifference to the ceiling cornice.

"There was some sort of a common-law wife, I understand."

"So I believe, sir."

Mr. Chubb waited a few more moments, said
"Mmm," and faced the room. He folded the Flaxborough *Citizen* neatly and held it out for Purbright to
take. "I suppose," he said, "that this makes her a common-law widow."

The funeral will take place tomorrow (Saturday) at
Flaxborough Crematorium, following a service at
Mumblesby Parish Church, conducted by the Vicar,

*the Rev. D. Kiverton, M.A. Arrangements have been
entrusted to Messrs. K. Bradlaw and Son Ltd., under-
takers, of Bride Street, Flaxborough.*

"Oh, bloody hell!"

The sheafs of polytropulene gladioli trembled in
their urns, and brass tinkled in the tall case of coffin-
handle samples opposite the door. A stained-glass
hatch opened in the wall behind the long mahogany
counter to disclose the almost exactly spherical head of
a young man, steamy-faced, prematurely bald, with
protuberant, anxious eyes and a nineteen-thirties film-
star moustache.

"Now what's wrong, Father?" the young man asked.
There was reproof in his tone; in his hand, which trembled, a chisel.

"You'd think they could get the sodding initial right
for once. They've only to look at the advert."

"The paper's always getting things wrong. You know
that. It's not worth working up your blood pressure."

Mr. Bradlaw, Sr., correct initials N.A., tapped the
offending column with his foot rule so angrily that the
page ruptured. "And just look at that. *Entrusted.* 'Arrangements have been *entrusted.*' That's what it says.
Entrusted." He looked up. "Of course, you know what
they're getting at?"

The undertaker's general construction bore close resemblance to that of his son. They were both portly, of
about the same height, and distinctly roundheaded,
with only a little pouch of a chin to mark the boundary
between face and neck. Each had high colour, but to
the son's there was more shine. The father's baldness,
too, lacked lustre; the scalp now looked a size too big
and it was pallid and deeply wrinkled, as if it had been
folded away for a long time in some dark cupboard.

"They're not getting at anything, Father. You're too
damn sensitive for your own good."

Mr. Bradlaw's eyes bulged and their lids went into a rapid blink. "Just you watch the language, boy," he admonished. His voice became husky. "You don't have to spare my feelings, Melville. I suppose it's nice to be 'entrusted' with things. I ought to be grateful. Old Nab the Lag. Alias K."

"Father, for heaven's sake! That was twenty years ago."

Mr. Bradlaw conveyed his opinion of time's healing powers in a short, humourless laugh. He then looked at his watch and reached beneath the counter for the wing collar and black silk tie that he had discarded in order to read the inaccuracies and innuendos of the Flaxborough *Citizen* in greater comfort, reassumed them with a single lasso-like movement, and made for the door leading to the street.

At the door, he turned.

"Did you ring Alf Blossom about the extra Daimler?"

"It's in the yard now. Oh, by the way . . ."

Melville's face disappeared from the hatch. After a few moments he came through the door from the workshop. He was holding a tangle of broad white ribbon.

"Nobody thought to say anything. Good job I noticed."

Nab Bradlaw snatched the ribbon. He said, "Jesus!" so tightly that it sounded like *Cheeses;* then, "What in hell does he think we're running—a bloody honeymoon hotel?"

His son held out his hand. "I'll get Betty to roll it up; then it can be put in the Daimler when it gets back from the Crem."

For answer, Bradlaw stuffed Mr. Blossom's tribute to Hymen into a sample cremation casket. "Have it dyed first thing Monday. The bearers' hats could do with jigging up a bit."

Melville looked shocked. "You can't *pinch* it. That stuff costs the earth."

"Well, it'll teach Alf Blossom not to *entrust* me with his jaunting gear another time, won't it, boy? The trouble with Alf's garage is that the boss has a one-track mind. That's no way to run a decent business."

"I don't see that hiring wedding cars gives him a one-track mind, as you put it."

Mr. Bradlaw, Sr., lowered his head and regarded Melville with melancholy admonition. "Don't you, boy? Don't you *really?*" He sighed, and went out into Bride Street.

CHAPTER 2

The village of Mumblesby—or, to give it its full name, Mumblesby Overmarsh with Ganby—had been a ruined hamlet a quarter of a century before. Its church had begun to moulder through disuse; half the houses were empty; the watermill by the choked stream was broken-wheeled and roofless. A few agricultural labourers, obedient to the calls of farmers Benjamin Croll, Arthur Pritty, and the Gash brothers, still lived in tied cottages with their sad-faced wives and a flock of timid, staring, fleet-footed children, but they had seen the arrival of the first of the great machines, like green and yellow dinosaurs, that soon would replace them in the fields. The vicar of that time, an incredibly ancient man, was walled up with his dog, housekeeper and bottles of linctus in the grey, moss-streaked parsonage, unseen by his parishioners except once a week when the housekeeper changed his bedclothes. Then, for a little while, the old man could be glimpsed sitting at the window of a downstairs room, wrapped in a sheet, as if hopeful of a place in the next hearse that might chance along. There was no traffic, though, past the parsonage in those days, either to the overgrown churchyard or, in the opposite direction, along the broad footpath to the Red Lion Inn, which the farmers could reach more conveniently in their Daimlers, Jaguars and Mercedes by the main road.

Today, Mumblesby was a village rescued and transformed. The church boasted a congregation once more, albeit a small one; the inn, a merry company (it had been renamed the Barleybird). Most of the cottages had been rebuilt and enlarged, some quite extravagantly. The millhouse was a restaurant. The primitive little school on the corner of Church Lane had become Gallery Ganby, where one could scarcely swing a chequebook without knocking down a spinning wheel or a warming pan. As for Mumblesby Manor, in 1960 as derelict as the squirearchy whose horses, dogs and women it once had housed, Rich Dick Loughbury's money and the fancifulness of his builder—a Mr. Ned Snell, cousin of the deputy town clerk of Flaxborough—had restored the fabric and embellished it with enough bows and bottle-glass to make it look like a Hollywood set for *Pride and Prejudice.*

The transfiguration of Mumblesby was, not unnaturally, the topic of conversation between Miss Lucy Teatime and her business associate, Mr. Edgar Harrington, when their motorcar drew into the village marketplace and halted facing the house of the deceased solicitor. They did not alight immediately, but sat at ease, gazing at the pristine brickwork, the flawless white paint, the elegant little skirt of railing before the front door.

"It is a saddening thought," said Miss Teatime, "that most of these changes have come about in what I suppose I am in the habit of calling 'my time.'"

"Since you came here from London, you mean?"

"Do you know, Edgar, it is all of fourteen years." She turned to him, her eyes suddenly wide.

"I don't believe it."

"True, alas. I emigrated, as one might say, in nineteen sixty-seven."

Mr. Harrington seemed to be doing a sum, but all he said was, "Harrods."

The faraway look in Miss Teatime's eyes faltered,

but only for a second. "I, too, have known bereavement," she murmured.

"Uncle Macnamara?" suggested Mr. Harrington, with every indication of concern. She made no reply. "But he is, ah, with us again now, surely?" he persisted, gently.

"Perhaps we should make our presence known at the house of mourning," suggested Miss Teatime, removing the key from the ignition. At once, her companion left the car and was opening her door before she could put the key in her handbag.

She gave a little smile of gratification. "What a nice mover you are, Edgar."

Mr. Harrington lightly supported her elbow until she stood on the broad-paved marketplace. The support was a courtesy but in no degree a requirement. Miss Teatime, in her own, slightly old-world way, was a nice mover too, even if she entertained private doubts of her capacity these days to outdistance a determined store detective.

They walked to the front door. Miss Teatime glanced at a squat, not very clean black Ford van parked a few yards away. "Oh, dear—tradesmen," she said, and looked for a bell push.

There was none. Choice lay between a laurel-wreath knocker in forged iron and, suspended from a little gallows at the side of the door, a brass stable bell. Edgar briskly wielded the knocker.

It was the owner of the van who opened the door.

"Yes?" whispered Mr. Bradlaw. He was in full kit. In the breast pocket of the cutaway coat were his folded rule and, tucked beside it, a pair of thin black cotton gloves.

Miss Teatime leaned confidentially towards him. "Callers," she breathed. "Old acquaintance. Pay respect." A wisp of handkerchief hovered a moment by

the corner of her mouth. Mr. Bradlaw quite liked the
suggestion of fragrance that reached him. He did not
know that it was called *Liaison plus tard.*

After brief consideration, the undertaker made a
movement with his head indicative of inner rooms.
"You know Mr. Loughbury's, er . . ." (he was whisper-
ing still) "his . . . you know the lady, do you?"

Miss Teatime allowed a watery smile to break
through her grief. "I believe that to understand is to
know," she said. "Don't you?"

Before Mr. Bradlaw could think of a reply adequate
to such profundity, he realised that the lady and gentleman had both stepped past him into the house.

"Who's that?" A woman's voice, not far off, cheery
and with a certain roughness. Youngish. Decidedly
local accent.

Mr. Bradlaw felt the back of his head with full palm,
as if deciding whether it was ripe enough. He looked at
Miss Teatime. "You'd better go through," he whispered.

The coffin was the first thing they saw. Set upon
draped trestles in the centre of the big light room, it
dominated everything else. Not for the first time, Miss
Teatime wondered at the sheer bulk of what Mr. Bradlaw called, almost affectionately, one of his "overcoats." One expected something about the length and
girth of its occupant with just a bit added on so as not
to look mean. In the event, the thing was overpowering
—not so much a box as a blockhouse. Why so *deep?* All
that wood incongruously new-looking, unnaturally
glossy . . . rather like toffee . . .

"Have you come to see him?"

The question was put flatly but with a hint of
shyness. A girl with slight physique and rather dingy
clothes was standing by an open cabinet at the far side
of the room.

"I'm sorry?" Mr. Harrington assumed an expression of anxiety to please, tempered by hardness of hearing. Miss Teatime took over. "I rather think that will not be necessary, my dear," she said.

The girl shrugged. She had thin but not weak shoulders. The arms, too, were thin, more so than the wrists promised; they, like the ankles disclosed by ragged grey flannel slacks, had been hardened and thickened by work.

She came nearer. An open, fresh-complexioned face; straight, light hair, randomly brushed; narrow nose and pale lips; eyes grey, interested, bold and wary at the same time. Narrow also the lively neck. Age somewhere between thirty-five and forty. Miss Teatime saw a girl; Edgar Harrington, a woman.

"You can have a look if you want," the girl offered again. "Nab won't mind. I mean, if you're re*la*tions . . ." Bradlaw, who had followed them in, stepped past them busily. Suddenly there was a screwdriver in his hand.

Miss Teatime shook her head. She touched his arm. "Oh, no, it is most kind of you, but . . ." (she groped for the prescribed formula) "but we would rather remember him as he was."

The girl glanced quickly from one to the other. She gave her nose a rabbit-twitch of puzzlement. "Hell, he's not gone *off*, if that's what you're worried about."

Miss Teatime held out her hand. The girl seized it forthrightly. Her smile prevailed over nervousness; it was diffident, boyish. She heard out the introductions and said: "I'm Mrs. Loughbury. Zoe. Well, Zoe Claypole, actually. But Dick had a sort of special licence thing going." She made a mock-posh face at Bradlaw. "The neighbours, don't you know."

Mr. Bradlaw took his leave after rehearsing the rest of the day's programme in solemn undertone. Zoe

watched the departure of his van. It made a lot of noise
and a lot of smoke and seemed to be difficult to steer.

"He's very kind, you know," the girl said, half to herself. "More than need go with the job."

She turned from the window. "Right, now we can
have a drink. I don't dare get it out while Nab's here.
They reckon he'll even sup embalming fluid."

Zoe crossed to a walnut corner cupboard from which
she drew out and flourished a pair of bottles. "There's
all sorts. Just say what you fancy." She scrutinised one
bottle narrowly against the light. "Christ, looks like a
urine sample." Then, brightening, "How about a
sherry? There's a nice one here that's not a bit sour.
Poor Dickie thought it was terrible, but he stuck to
whiskey mostly." She rummaged more deeply. "Hey,
here's some of that lovely yucky green stuff. A boy-
friend of mine used to give it to me mixed with
Guinness. Jeez . . ."

"Whiskey, I think," said Miss Teatime, "would be
very acceptable." She glanced at Mr. Harrington, who
said quickly, "Yes, yes indeed."

Zoe said, "Half a tick," and fetched three tumblers
from another room. She half-filled two of them, pouring the whiskey with bold dispatch, like disinfectant.
Into the third glass, more lovingly, she slurped sweet
sherry.

Miss Teatime raised her tumbler. "To the dear departed." Her companion made a reverent murmur.

"Cheers," said Zoe, then, as if on afterthought, went
again to the cupboard and topped up her sherry with
crème de menthe. She winked fondly at the coffin lid
and took a sip. She closed her eyes. "Bloody sight better than with Guinness."

Miss Teatime looked about her. "You have a very
beautiful home, Mrs. Loughbury." Edgar pursed his
lips and nodded.

Zoe sighed. "I'm very lucky, really."

Not half, reflected Mr. Harrington, eyeing a group of enamelled and silver-gilt snuffboxes. He also noted the pair of Meissen figures that set off a rosewood table (Florentine?—he thought it probable) and the miniature, aglow in its collar of elaborate gilt, depicting one of the children of Louis XVI. Concerning most of the pictures he was less confident, but one—whose gaiety of colour and exquisite geometrics proclaimed Klee— struck him as almost certainly an original.

Zoe saw him looking. She pouted at it disparagingly.

"Like it, do you?"

He said nothing but peered closer. It was, it had to be.

"Reckon I could do better myself," said Zoe. "The trouble with getting presents from people is that you've got to keep them where they can be seen."

Miss Teatime joined Edgar in regarding the picture. "It was a gift, was it?" she inquired indifferently over her shoulder.

"Not to me." Zoe seemed to find that notion amusing. "To Dickie. Instead of a fee, I expect. He was soft about bills. Poor duck."

"Ah, like doctors."

"Pardon me?"

"Doctors," explained Miss Teatime, "once were known to accept payment in kind. Before the National Health Service. I had not realised that solicitors might find themselves similarly placed."

Zoe said, "Oh yes, Mr. Loughbury quite often got presents. That could have been a reason."

"I rather like it, you know," said Miss Teatime. It sounded like a concession.

"You don't!"

"Yes, I do. In a way."

"Perhaps," put in Mr. Harrington, "Mrs. Loughbury

would consider selling it. If she does not care for it, I mean. I cannot pretend that I do either, but if you would permit me . . ." His hand, wallet-seeking, insinuated itself beneath the lapel of his jacket.

Miss Teatime regarded him smilingly for a moment, then: "Stop it, Edgar; you look like Napoleon. That picture's market value is something in the region of eighteen thousand pounds, and well you know it." She turned to Zoe. "I'm sorry, my dear, I have not had him long and he is not yet house-trained."

The girl was staring incredulously at the painting. "Eighteen *thousand*," she echoed.

"Thereabouts. The gentleman who painted it was very famous. He was called Mr. Klee." Edgar was now the young person's guide to great art.

Zoe nudged him. "You were trying to take me to the cleaners, old mate." Her forefinger jabbed sharply into the expensive suiting in the region of Edgar's diaphragm. "*Were*n't you?" Her expression had lost none of its amiability.

Edgar winced. He appeared to contract. "I was joking."

For a second, Zoe's regard wandered to the coffin. "Dickie was a bit of a joker," she said, gently. "But about money—never."

They talked of the future. Zoe said she had no plans to move to a smaller house, or to move from the village at all. Her late husband had enjoyed good social connexions, of which she, Zoe, was anxious to take advantage now that she had the opportunity. (Dickie had always tended to be overconsiderate, bless him, with the result that she had been somewhat isolated from Mumblesby society.) There were lots of things she wanted to help with: the church garden pageant, the Conservative gala, the Gentry and Yeomanry Association, and, of course, the Hunt—that especially.

The solicitor's choice of whiskey proved to be very much to Miss Teatime's taste. Mr. Harrington, all further jests foresworn, was also now paying its virtues due attention.

The past was touched upon.

"Were you brought up in these parts, Mrs. Loughbury?" Miss Teatime inquired.

"Zoe."

"Very well. Zoe."

"No, not round here. Flax. My old man kept a pub, as a matter of fact."

Mr. Harrington looked pleased to hear it. So did Miss Teatime, who asked, "Which one?" and insisted that she be addressed henceforth as Lucy.

"Oh, a real grotty old dump. Saracen's Head."

"Off Church Street?"

"That's it."

"A delightful inn," exclaimed Miss Teatime. "How can you call it grotty? I remember your father from my first days in Flaxborough. Fred—am I right? He and some other gentlemen in the bar taught me the game of dominoes." She turned to Edgar. "What a small world, is it not?"

Zoe was no less moved by the coincidence. "Christ! It was you, was it? Dad often talked about this old bird with a five-pound-note voice who pretended she didn't know a blank from a six-spot and then took ten whiskies in one session off the poor old sod." Admiration shone in her eyes.

"Is your father still alive?"

"He passed away last February."

"Oh, dear."

"Mum's still on the go. They were going to put her into that Twilight Close place, but she wasn't having any. Dick was very good. He got the new landlord at the Saracen's to let Mum stay on in a flat of her own."

"It must be—must have been—advantageous to have so persuasive a husband, Zoe."

The relict smiled reflectively. "There were no flies on Dickie." She looked up. "Oh, I beg your pardon, Lucy; p'raps that sounds like talking disrespectfully of the dead, you being a friend of his, but it is true. I mean, not *sharp,* nothing like that, but . . ." She plucked the air.

"Shrewd," supplied Miss Teatime.

"Yep." And Zoe's raised fingers snapped. "That's it. A real gentleman, but always on the ball."

Miss Teatime said they would have to be going. It had been most kind of Zoe to allow them to mark in a personal way the sad conclusion of a long acquaintanceship.

Zoe collected their glasses. She saw them to the door.

"Glad to have met you." She stood on the step and waved cheerily as they entered the car.

Miss Teatime, who was driving, waved back. Mr. Harrington held a limp hand at shoulder level for a second. Then they were out of the marketplace and on the Flaxborough road.

"I like Zoe," stated Miss Teatime, firmly.

Mr. Harrington made a murmur of qualified agreement. "There is," he said, "something rather refreshing about the articulate working-class girl, *rara avis* as she is. A mixture of eagerness and naïveté."

Miss Teatime smiled at the road ahead. "You supposed, did you not, that Zoe was eager to get rid of that painting, and naïve enough to part with it to the first person to turn up with a chequebook and a Marlborough accent."

"I should not have put it quite in those words."

"No, perhaps I express myself vulgarly, but you really must make greater effort to remember that you are no longer on the Bucks and Berks circuit, Edgar."

"I am scarcely likely to forget it," said Edgar, bitterly.

"Ah, but you do, dear boy, you do. You are progressing nicely in general, but certain differences you have not fully grasped. The most important is that the rich in London, though unprincipled, are at pains to conceal the fact, which makes them vulnerable; whereas a certain cachet attaches to knavery in these parts, even at the higher levels of society."

"I still think that Zoe—is that what she was called, Zoe?—would have parted with that Klee if you had not chopped my legs off so obligingly."

Miss Teatime gave a little laugh. "Oh, Edgar, your feelings are hurt!" She took one hand from the wheel and patted his thigh. "Now, if you promise not to sulk, I shall tell you something that I saw this morning and you did not. It was lying on that music stool beside the walnut cabinet."

"It being . . . ?" Mr. Harrington was looking monumentally unconcerned.

"A Brownlow trade and auction guide. Now, then, by whom would you rather have had your legs chopped off—me or Zoe?"

CHAPTER 3

"Your name, please, sir?" The request came from a young man with carefully combed hair and stylish eyeglasses who held a pencil in one hand and in the other a small notebook with entries in disproportionately large writing.

"Purbright. Detective Inspector W. W for Walter."

Behind the young man's glasses, a sudden alertness, excitement, hope. He clawed down the name and got the spelling wrong. Purbright, stooping a little patiently, gave it again, letter by letter. He always had considered name-taking at funerals a rotten job.

The reporter, too recent a recruit to Flaxborough journalism to have suspected guile in the decision to "let" him undertake so important an assignment, wondered if this tall, kindly man with something still of corn colour in his greying hair would confide in him the nature of his inquiries. Hanky-panky with the will? An insurance fraud? Arrest imminent, perhaps? An autopsy? Oh, God, let there be an exhumation . . .

"Representing," Purbright added clearly and slowly, "the Chief Constable, Mr. Harcourt Chubb."

"Oh." The young man looked disappointed. He turned a page.

"Two B's in Chubb," Purbright said. Bowing his head, he passed through the low doorway from the porch into the darkness of the church.

Next in line was Mr. Ernest Hideaway, the estate agent and town councillor, a hearty, bald-headed man

with lips so prominent and restless with incipient jests
they conferred upon him an unfortunate resemblance
to a foraging cod. "You know me, boy," he said to the
reporter (who didn't), and with a wink he was gone,
followed by Mrs. Hideaway, who whispered im-
periously as she passed: "And *don't* forget the O.B.E.
this time."

"Who was that, please?" the young man inquired
piteously of a tall, wooden-visaged gentleman wearing
huge black spectacles. But the doyen of Flaxborough
solicitors heard him not, nor halted his stately progress
through the porch. "Mr. Justin Scorpe," he boomed in
transit. "Representing the Law Society."

The young man scribbled it down, adding "O.B.E."
and "Mrs."—an endowment that would do nothing the
following Friday to help discount a long-cherished
public suspicion of scandalous liaison between wid-
ower Scorpe and Mrs. Bertha Hideaway.

Within the parish church of St. Dennis the Martyr,
between forty and fifty people had assembled already.
A dozen or so were Mumblesby residents; most of the
others had come out from Flaxborough. Their association with Richard Loughbury had been, in the main,
professional rather than personal, and they wore now
the air not so much of mourners as of shareholders,
meeting for the declaration of an already known final
dividend.

Purbright for a while loitered unobtrusively at the
back of the church. He recognised most of those who
had been shown to seats. Clay, headmaster of Flaxborough Grammar School, the pink, tight skin of his
face reflecting the altar candlelight; old Noddy Durham, the auctioneer, head going like a woodpecker's;
Fergusson, police surgeon; Clapper Buxton, Loughbury's confidential clerk; a woman called Mrs.
Ackroyd, who did the secretarial work and funeral-at-

tending for the chairmen of several Flaxborough Town
Council committees.

Mr. Bradlaw's ushers had separated the Flaxborough
and Mumblesby contingents so that the smaller—the
locals—sat on the right of the central aisle behind the
two empty pews reserved for members of the family.
No communication of any kind passed from one side to
the other, once Mr. Hideaway's salutations had been
repulsed by cold stares. The general feeling in both
camps now seemed to be one of mild, resigned bore-
dom, in keeping with the sounds that were being
gently toothpasted forth by an invisible organist.

After about ten minutes, the ushers filed out of the
church preparatory to doubling as bearers. Purbright
moved nearer the assembly and took a corner seat in
the shelter of a pillar. Soon there reached him from
behind a shuffling sound. Also a cold draught.

"I am the resurrection and the life . . ."

Ponderously and reluctantly, the members of the
congregation clambered to their feet. They sounded
like a score of Counts of Monte Cristo emerging from
the Château d'Yf.

As soon as the procession drew level with him, the
inspector tilted his bowed head so as to see who was
going by.

The Vicar of Mumblesby—or so Purbright assumed
him to be, for he was a recent incumbent—looked surprisingly athletic as he made his slow stride in skirt and
cassock. He intoned the words of the service loudly
and musically, and looked directly upward every now
and again as if to make sure that God was paying attention.

Purbright let the coffin slide past his line of sight and
awaited, not without a degree of vulgar curiosity, a first
view of Richard Loughbury's widow.

He was disappointed.

The coffin was followed by three mourners only, all men.

They wore short, firm-shouldered black overcoats, and from the right hand of each hung a black, new-looking hat. The hats looked disproportionately big.

One man, older than the others, walked slightly in the lead. His face wore a sternness that Purbright fancied expressive of annoyance rather than grief. A brother of the dead man? Purbright believed he had heard mention of one. The others, perhaps, were his sons, nephews of "Rich Dick!" The inspector looked for family resemblance. The younger men, though, kept their gaze resolutely on their own slow-pacing feet.

Where, then, was the late solicitor's consort: the wife, common-law or otherwise, of his bosom?

Purbright was not alone in being exercised by this question. Outside the church, a worried undertaker was interrogating the driver of the hearse.

"But, Christ, you *must* have seen her. She was at the house."

"Not when I came away, she wasn't."

Mr. Bradlaw, pop-eyed with agitation, thrust stubby fingers through imaginary hair. "I've known some cockups in my time, but we've never mislaid a bloody widow before."

"P'raps she went a different way round. P'raps she's in the church now."

Bradlaw regarded the driver with a mixture of pity and ferocity and scuttled back into the porch, where he sat and attempted to compose himself with the aid of a slug of gin, conjured from the tail of his coat. He was still hunched disconsolately on the stone bench when he heard footsteps hastening across gravel and some distressful deep breathing. In the doorway appeared a short, plump woman, bespectacled and red-faced, grey hair straggling from beneath a Sunday-best hat. She seized Bradlaw's arm and brought her face close. Bradlaw tried to conceal his recent indulgence by breathing sideways out of the corner of his mouth, then saw that she was too upset to notice.

"You'll never," she gasped, "guess what they've done, Mr. Bradlaw. Never." She straightened up and made sure her hat was still on. Then she glared at the door beyond which the intoning of the vicar could be heard. "You'll have to tell them to stop. If you don't, *I* shall."

Bradlaw, getting to his feet, saw her reach for the latch. He hastened to her side.

"You can't just burst in there, Mrs. Claypole. The service has started."

"It's disgraceful!" she said. "Him not in the ground yet, and them doing that to her in her own house."

Bradlaw put his hands on her shoulders and tried to calm and reroute her at the same time. "If only you'll tell me what's happened," he pleaded.

"Happened!" repeated Mrs. Claypole, explosive with indignation. "You'd better ask them in there what's happened!"

The woman was immovable. Worse, Bradlaw realised that she had managed to unlatch the door and wedge it partly open with her hip. He got one eye to the aperture and peered towards the congregation. There were pale blurs in the gloom. Turned, what's-going-on faces. Oh, God, and here was one of them coming out . . .

Inspector Purbright, whose unwise election to sit further from the front than anyone else made him the clearest possible candidate for dealing with trouble at the back, shut the door quietly but firmly behind him and besought the lady to tell him her troubles.

"It's my Zoe," declared Mrs. Claypole. "They've locked her up, those devils have. In her own house."

Mr. Bradlaw remarked tetchily that she might have said so before . . . "Mrs. Claypole," he explained to Purbright, "is the mother of the lady who looked after Mr. Loughbury." His tone lowered a fraction. "I was rather expecting her—this lady's daughter, I mean—to be in the church. That was the arrangement."

Mrs. Claypole took a great gulp of air. "Expecting her to be in church!" She turned to Purbright and regarded him narrowly. "You're a policeman, aren't you?"

"I am, yes."

She pointed at the door. "That ought to be stopped at once."

For a moment Purbright appeared to be giving the proposal serious consideration. Bradlaw gaped and lost some colour; the vision of a squad of constables commandeering one of his "occasions" (as he called them) had been a recurrent waking nightmare ever since the Carobleat cremation scandal in the fifties.

But the inspector counselled instead that the most sensible, and doubtless the kindest, course would be to secure the release of the detainee.

After a token show of further truculence, Mrs. Claypole allowed him to lead her to the churchyard gate and along the path to the Manor House.

Mr. Bradlaw glanced aloft in pious commiseration, and took another quick swig of gin.

Purbright and Mrs. Claypole made entry to the Manor House through a conservatory at the side, where Mrs. Claypole disinterred a key from a pot of compost. They passed through a big double kitchen and along a cork-tiled corridor hung with framed illustrations from ancient cookery books.

On reaching the hall, Mrs. Claypole made at once for the stairs. Purbright glanced about him as he followed. He saw lots of white doors with sharply defined panelling. The ceiling was set about with mouldings meticulously restored. Everywhere, whites and ivories: they invested the central well with a cool pearl-like glow.

"All right, love!" bellowed Mrs. Claypole, halfway up the staircase. "We're coming!"

At the top, she led Purbright to a passageway off the main corridor and on a slightly lower level. She indicated a door, then called out again at undiminished volume: "Are you there, love?"

The cry produced an echoing resonance. Bathroom, thought Purbright. A woman's voice within said something he didn't catch.

"Right, then!" Mrs. Claypole straightened up and stepped to the left of the door. She looked at Purbright with an expression of confidence and encouragement. He realised that he stood to be favoured with the role of shoulder-charging rescuer.

"I think," he suggested, "that a key would be best, if we can find one."

Mrs. Claypole bent to the door and yelled: "Is there a key, duckie?"

This time the reply was audible. "Oh, Mum, of course there's a bloody key. How could I be locked in if there wasn't?"

"I shall look around, if I may," Purbright said. "Keys often are interchangeable."

Mrs. Claypole nodded. She was looking much more cheerful. Better for her than funerals, Purbright thought. He wandered off, looking at keyholes.

No other doors were locked, it seemed. Few, though, were without keys. Purbright began collecting them, after first lightly pencilling matching numbers on keys and doorposts.

Several rooms were empty or occupied only by pieces of furniture obviously intended for deployment elsewhere. Some of Loughbury's acquisitions in the antique market, assumed Purbright. Most were clearly of fine workmanship and authentic styling. They included a richly carved wooden chair with a very long back, a grandfather clock, the face of which was full of suns and moons, and a curious little lidded table with what looked like tea caddies suspended beneath.

Three bedrooms were furnished for use, expensively but not unconventionally. The largest, containing a double bed, unmade, and a dressing table covered with bottles and part-packets of chocolate and sweets, smelled of scent.

Scent. Purbright sniffed. Scent and . . . not *kippers*, surely? He extracted the key from the door and made his pencil marks. Amblesby, he mused, the old Flaxborough coroner, used to nibble kippers in bed. But they hardly qualified, even by Mrs. Claypole's homely standards, as funeral meats. Smoked salmon, now . . .

He swung about, suddenly alarmed, and saw it almost at once. A thin feather of smoke, curling from the edge of a door in the opposite wall of the bedroom.

Purbright strode past the bed, reached for the door's polished brass handle, then paused. He touched the metal. It was cool. So was the door itself. Guardedly, he opened it a few inches.

There was a fair amount of smoke in the room beyond, but it was by no means impenetrable. Purbright saw no sign of flame. The room was much smaller than the bedroom; he supposed it to be a dressing room. Clothing certainly it contained—a pile of dresses and underwear in the further corner, smouldering steadily. He pulled the door shut.

Purbright hurried back to a second bathroom which he had noted a few minutes earlier. He set the bath taps running and soaked the largest towel he could see.

When he returned to the dressing room, the first flames were emerging sulkily from the clothing. He cast the wet towel over the pile, and gathered as much as he could in a tight mass within it, then ran to the bath.

After two more trips, nothing remained in the dressing room but a scattering of blackened scraps of cloth and some fragments melted upon the casing of a small electric heater. Over this somebody must have draped the clothes in ignorance of its being switched on.

The smell of burning accompanied Purbright when, at last, he presented himself at the side of Mrs. Claypole and prepared to work through his key collection. She broke off the conversation she had been holding with her daughter, stared at Purbright and sniffed accusingly. "There's something on fire."

He introduced the first key and wiggled it about with great concentration, his eye level with it. "On fire? No, no, nothing's on fire. Look, hold these, do you mind?" He selected a second key from the bundle and handed her the rest. "Bit of cloth smouldering. Out now. Nothing to get worried about." He squinted along the barrel of the next key.

"Cloth?" echoed Mrs. Claypole. "What cloth? Smouldering? Where?"

"Out now," muttered Purbright. Without looking at her, he held up his hand for another key.

It fitted and, with some resistance, turned.

For the first time since getting involved in the business, Purbright found himself wondering what would confront him when the door opened. He heard, as if it were an old recording, the never-believed claim of Detective Constable Harper: *And there she was, Sarge, absolutely starkers!*

"I think you'll find you can get in now, Mrs. Claypole." He turned and stood gazing back along the passage.

Zoe was greeted by her mother as if she had just

been winched down from the top of the Empire State Building.

"Oh, Mum, shut up, for Christ's sake." She pulled straight her modest black frock (Detective Constable Harper would have been much disappointed) and grimaced at the bathroom mirror.

"Who was it, then?" inquired her mother. "Who locked that door, Zoe? Who was it locked that door? That's what I want to know."

Zoe spotted Purbright's modestly withdrawn figure; he had moved to the corner of the main corridor. She pointed and made a Who's-that? face.

"You know who it is," whispered her mother. "You saw him that day when our Douglas was up in court. He was the one with those papers."

"Oh, shit, not a policeman?"

"Listen, my girl, you'd be in a bad way if it wasn't for him, whether he's a policeman or not. As a matter of fact"—a note of self-congratulation—"he's an inspector." Mrs. Claypole turned and raised her voice to normal: "Excuse me, er . . . Mr. . . ."

Purbright walked back. He made a small bow to Zoe. "Are you all right, Mrs. Loughbury?" There had been no equivocation in his choice of phrase. Zoe smiled her gratitude.

The mother produced a smile also, but it was a proprietary one. "Mrs. Claypole-Loughbury, actually," she explained to Purbright, and looked as if she were going to say some more.

The younger woman took her arm brusquely. "Come on, Mum; I've been perched on the edge of that bloody bath so long that I've got a crease in my arse."

They moved off towards the stairs.

Purbright spoke, levelly but earnestly, about his discovery in the dressing room. Zoe agreed that, now that he'd mentioned it, there certainly was a bloody pong in the air. Mrs. Claypole, at full throttle of alarm once more, repeatedly demanded who had been so wicked as to set fire to the house.

Purbright showed them the ruined but now harmless tangle of charred clothes in the bath. The sight moved Mrs. Claypole to new transports of indignation. Then he led them to the bedroom and its annex.

"The heater is off now, of course," he said, "but I don't doubt that it was the cause of the trouble. It—and a certain degree of carelessness, I'm afraid." He really did sound regretful; there was nothing admonitory in his tone.

Mrs. Claypole exercised no such restraint. "Zoe, you little idiot! What on earth were you thinking about? All those lovely things. And the whole house could have gone up. Then what would you have done?"

"Gone up with it, I suppose." The retort lacked spike; Zoe had only half-listened to her mother. She stood regarding the heater, its bronze enamel streaked and crusted with black, rather as if her mind were elsewhere.

Purbright put no questions. But while Mrs. Claypole peered, clucking, at evidence of near-disaster, he watched the younger woman.

After a few moments, she looked up. The inspector followed her gaze.

He saw, set high into the wall, what appeared to be a stoutly constructed birdcage.

Almost at once, her regard moved, met his own, then fell. "You must be thinking I'm a pretty stupid cluck."

Purbright shrugged. "We all do silly things at times. When we're under stress, especially." He looked at his watch. "You'd better get back to the church. I'll just hang on here a minute to make sure everything's safe." He glanced from mother to daughter. "Provided you don't have any objection, of course."

Mrs. Claypole said: "It's very kind of you, Inspector." She shuddered at the heater. "Even the thought of fire scares me to death. Just the *thought*." She pulled Zoe's arm through her own. "Come on, then: I don't know *what* they'll be thinking in church."

"Getting out for a drink, I should think. What else?" Zoe allowed Mrs. Claypole to lead her from the room. But in the instant of passing through the door she glanced once again at the cage on the wall.

CHAPTER 4

As soon as Zoe and her mother arrived at the church, Mr. Bradlaw took them into his personal custody and conducted them slowly and with dignity up the central aisle. The Reverend Alan Kiverton, noticing the new procession, stopped praying. He took delivery of the two ladies and shepherded them to the front pew, where he proceeded to signify by gestures regretful but mandatory that the three gentlemen already installed should yield their places.

Mr. Stan Loughbury, wholesale ironmonger, and his two sons remained motionless. They stared stonily ahead. The rest of the congregation, sensing a more than ordinary case of bloodymindedness, craned and rustled.

Five seconds went by. Mr. Kiverton, in truth, dismayed but committed now to relegation, summoned facial expressions in pairs: anger and conciliation, blame and forgiveness, exasperation and patience—rather like a machine designed to consume its own smoke.

All this Anglican diplomacy had no effect. The situation, it seemed to the now thoroughly intrigued onlookers, was one of siege.

Then, so suddenly that no one afterwards could quite recall the course of events, the two younger recalcitrants were rising painfully to their feet. At a list suggestive of a strong side wind, they quit the pew. Behind them, gripping an ear of each, was Zoe.

Mr. Loughbury, Sr., seemed to be considering a reprisal of some kind; then he, too, abandoned the pew. Zoe immediately pushed her mother into one of the vacated places and sat down herself, as bland of feature as a nun.

Mr. Kiverton remained standing where he was just long enough to feel assured that the Loughburys would not regroup for a counterattack, then went back to the altar steps and got a hymn started with his confident, declamatory tenor.

During the singing, the displaced mourners briefly conferred and then marched out in line, angrily brushing black hats on black sleeves. Mr. Bradlaw, who hated the slightest disruption of his arrangements, gloomily watched their departure in the direction of the car park and the Barleybird Inn.

He spoke to his son.

"That's that, then. Now there's no family at all. None of the other lots came, you know."

"Did you find out why?"

"Oh, I knew why, Son. Didn't have to ask."

"Because of her, was it?"

"Course it was."

"I don't see that it matters. His wife was dead. He could please himself."

Mr. Bradlaw snorted mirthlessly at this display of simplemindedness. "Oh dear, oh dear."

His son flushed. "Well, why not? What have his relations to get worked up about?"

A deep sigh. Words squeezed painfully past Mr. Bradlaw's exasperation. "Money, boy . . . *mon-ey!*"

The departure of Richard Loughbury's brother and nephews was noticed by Inspector Purbright as he looked out of one of the windows of the Manor House, but he did not interpret it in terms of family disagreement. It was, he supposed, simply a sign that the service was at an end. The cortège would soon be leaving for the crematorium at Flaxborough. There was not much time left in which he could convincingly claim to be taking precautions against fire breaking out again.

He already had searched thoroughly the bathroom in which Zoe had been locked. Its window, an old-fashioned guillotine, was painted shut at the bottom, and he doubted if the woman could have reached to slip a key out of the narrow gap near the ceiling. Of course, she might have hidden it beneath her own clothing.

Or was her mother's suggestion the true one? That someone in the corridor had turned the key while Zoe was washing, pocketed it and quietly rejoined the others downstairs as they were leaving for the church?

Purbright realised that either supposition could be justified. Here was a man's mistress who might well be deemed an upstart and an interloper by his family and friends. Rather than facing out their hostility at the funeral, she was not to be blamed for dodging the occasion by a small subterfuge.

Conversely, a relative who felt strongly opposed to her presence certainly could have contrived to forestall it by the same means.

In neither case, Purbright reminded himself, had there been infringement of the law, other than of a pretty footling kind.

So why was he now wasting time wandering from room to room in Mumblesby Manor when he could be on his way to what was left of Saturday afternoon in his own garden in Flaxborough?

It was the thought of the pile of smouldering clothes in the dressing room that disturbed him. Explanations came to mind readily enough, simple and perfectly reasonable explanations. Heaters did get switched on thoughtlessly, even accidentally. And, wrong as it was for clothes to get tossed over them, that did happen—especially when people were worried or in haste.

Reasonable explanations, certainly. As reasonable in their way as either of those alternative explanations of the locked door. On different days, or in different places, reasonable. But within the same hour, the same house?

For the fifth time, Purbright entered the small room where the fire had been. It contained little. Beneath the window was an openwork cane chest, half filled with bed linen. A matching cane chair stood between it and the electric heater. Next to the door leading into the passage was a glazed earthenware jar, two feet tall, from which protruded two very old golf clubs and a shooting stick. The only other portable object was a japanned deed box, much battered and bearing splashes of anciently spilled paint, its lid secured by a small and considerably newer-looking padlock. This box stood just behind the communicating door from the bedroom, as though it had been placed there as a stop.

All these things Purbright gave long, thoughtful scrutiny without disturbing them. Then he went over to the one object in the room for which he felt totally unable to account and began to examine it in detail.

He saw that "birdcage" was not, after all, a fitting description. A cage, yes—about eight inches square and standing an inch and a half out from the wall—but the bars were nearly a quarter of an inch thick, and made, he thought, of stainless steel. Behind this grille was glass, of what thickness Purbright could not judge, and behind the glass a recess had been cut into the wall to the depth of a brick.

The arrangement was of the kind within which a jeweller might display a single piece of such value as to require special precautions against theft or damage.

What Purbright saw in the recess, though, was not jewellery. It was a lump of wood. Roughly rectangular and four or five inches long, it looked as if it had been split away from a bigger whole. A card was propped against it. Purbright read the five words typed on the card: FRAGMENT OF THE TRUE CROSS.

The odd thing (if all this were not odd enough) was that he could see no way in which the exhibit might be withdrawn. All the bars were set solidly in cement. None was hinged. There was no sign of an opening at the back of the recess; in any case, even if one existed, it could be reached only by climbing some fifteen feet up an outside wall.

The "fragment" clearly had been intended to remain a permanent and inaccessible exhibit. Purbright shrugged and turned away; he was aware that the zeal of collectors was liable to outstrip rationality.

Cars were being started in the marketplace. The mourners, or some of them, would soon be on their way to Flaxborough for the short ceremony at the Crematorium. Others might be calling back at the house. Purbright had no wish to be trapped into giving account of himself.

Before leaving, he pulled the heater's plug from the wall socket. Then he took hold of the cane chair with the intention of moving it to a safer distance from the heater.

It was surprisingly heavy.

A number of underclothes had been heaped untidily in the chair. Purbright pulled one or two aside. He felt something hard. He removed more of the clothing and saw a squat, red-painted cylinder. It was a bottle of propane gas.

Cautiously, Purbright eased the valve open a fraction. There was an immediate lively hiss. He screwed the valve shut and carried the propane downstairs. He found the kitchen again and placed the bottle on a big wooden-topped table.

Near the window was a telephone. He rang Flaxborough Police Station.

Detective Sergeant Sidney Love sounded sympathetic. Funerals he considered only marginally less tedious than weddings, but at least they generally were over more quickly. To be delayed at one—and one, moreover, that was entirely someone else's pigeon—struck him as the worst kind of luck. Yes, of course he would tell Mrs. Purbright; and yes, he would go round to Market Street and ask if he might have a copy of the *Citizen's* list of mourners,

"What do you know about bottled gas, Sid? In particular, the difference between butane and propane?"

"Isn't butane the one for house heaters? I think propane's the high-pressure one. Welding, that sort of thing."

"I take it, then, that it would be pretty foolish to put a propane bottle on the fire."

Love thought, but was not sure, that he had been presented with a rhetorical question, so he returned an all-purpose answer in the form of a throaty puffing sound—a "pwhu-urr!"

"Oh, and Sid . . ."

"Yes?"

"When old Loughbury last submitted a list of the property in his house at Mumblesby, do you remember if it included a religious relic of some kind?"

"There was a chalice that he'd got marked up at a couple of thousand."

"Not a chalice," Purbright said. "A relic. Something supposedly holy."

"A bone?" Love suggested, dubiously.

"A bit of wood, actually." The inspector knew when he had hit a dead end.

"Don't recall any wood," said the sergeant.

"Never mind."

It was nearly an hour before Purbright heard a car draw up before the house and a key turn in the front door. He went at once into the hall.

Zoe, entering first, looked surprised. She was followed by her mother. Mrs. Claypole glanced at Purbright's feet. He wondered if he were suspected of having had them up on the furniture.

Zoe began to pull off her gloves. No one had spoken.

"I must apologise," Purbright said, "if I've overstayed my welcome but . . ."

Zoe interrupted him. "That's all right. Anytime." She stuffed her gloves into the pocket of her coat. "My God, I'm dying for a cuppa."

Mrs. Claypole said she would make one after she'd been upstairs. She began, ponderously, to climb them.

"I was saying, I'm sorry to be still here, but there is a matter I think I ought to talk to you about," Purbright said to Zoe.

"You'd better come in the lounge, then." She opened a door. "Is Mum to bring you a cup?"

He said that was kind of her. Zoe waved the inspector to a deep armchair. He stood by it, regarding her, waiting for her to sit.

When she moved to a chair, it was to kneel in it, one arm hanging over the back. The attitude put Purbright in mind of a schoolgirl too big for her age.

"I should like you to tell me," he began, "what ideas you have concerning this bathroom business." He saw a sudden upturn of the eyes in exasperation. "I am not asking without a very good reason."

"Oh, dear, trust my blessed mother to find a policeman without even looking. I should think you were the only one in ten miles."

"That's quite possible." He sounded rueful.

She smiled, then frowned, looking away. "Ideas? No, not specially. Bloody stupid trick. I suppose someone thought it was funny."

"An odd occasion, I should have thought, for practical jokes, Mrs. Loughbury? A funeral."

"Queer village." She said it without emphasis, almost dismissively.

"Is it, indeed?"

That won no response. He asked her: "How many people—other than Mr. Bradlaw and his staff—were in the house when you were getting ready to go to church?"

"Not very many." Zoe saw that a pencil and a piece of folded paper had got into the inspector's hand. She stared at them blankly.

"The names—do you remember them?"

"Does it matter? Don't tell me they've made locking doors a crime."

"Not in general, no. The people in the house, though —do you recall who they were?"

Memory cracked the impassivity of her face with a smile. "There was old Jehovah and his two witnesses. Dickie's brother from Chalmsbury. He always called him that. Old Jehovah. Stan, actually. Miserable old prick. I can't remember what the sons are called. They never came over until today, and that was too bloody soon."

"Zoe! Just you watch your language!" Mrs. Claypole, tractoring a laden tea tray into the room, paused to glare. "Whatever would your hubby have thought?" And her eyes switched to Purbright, as if in hope of his being privy to the opinions of the late solicitor.

"He wants to know who was here this morning," Zoe said to her mother.

Mrs. Claypole busied herself with pouring milk into three cups. Her "Oh?" was restrained.

"I told him Stan and the wet dreams. Who else was there? Mr. Croll. He was here, wasn't he, Mum?"

"Croll?" Purbright repeated.

"The farmer," said Zoe. "Ben. The one whose wife done herself in."

Again a frown of deep disapproval from Mrs. Claypole. "Zoe, there was no call for that." Purbright was beginning to wonder at what age her mother would deem Zoe brought up.

"Ah, yes," he said.

"Then there was Winnie Gash and Spen. They were both here."

"They're farmers too," Mrs. Claypole explained to Purbright. "Brothers, Winston and Spencer. They have a big place. Ever so big." She turned to her daughter. "Isn't it a big place, Zoe? The Gashes?"

"Are those gentlemen married?" Purbright inquired of Zoe.

"Oh, yes; both married."

"So there had been present the two brothers and their wives—is that right?"

Both women shook their heads. "No, no—not the wives. It was nearly harvest time. There would be too much to do."

"The husbands, then. Anyone else?"

"There was Mr. Palgrove and his wife. Len—that's Mr. Palgrove—he's got the restaurant, but it doesn't open until the evening," Zoe explained. "So they popped in for a sherry."

Purbright's brow raised very slightly as he made a note on his piece of paper.

Mrs. Claypole noticed.

"There was refreshments," she said, archly, "as I'm sure my daughter's late hubby would have wished."

"Mr. and Mrs. Leonard Palgrove," Purbright confirmed. "Anyone else?"

"Some more of his family were supposed to be coming," said Zoe, "but they never turned up. They was all told."

Mrs. Claypole smirked disapprovingly.

"Of course, the Flaxborough lot stayed pretty much together and went straight in the church," Zoe said. "The lawyers and councillors and that. Well, there wasn't room here for a full do. It was just friends from round about."

"Mr. Cork-Bradden," supplied Mrs. Claypole, with a touch of pride.

"Yes, that's right. Him and her ladyship." Zoe watched Purbright's pencil. "Hyphen," she said. "I suppose you could say he's the squire. Sort of. He goes hunting and all that, anyway. Churchwarden. Conservative Committee. *And* well heeled."

"Does he," the inspector asked, "have an E on his Cork?"

They did not know, but thought not.

Two more names came up. Mrs. Whybrow, summarised somewhat scantly by Zoe as "the horsey old cow Dickie used to screw tenants for"; and Mr. Raymond Bishop, who lodged with her in Church Lane.

"So, apart from yourselves and Mr. Bradlaw's people, there were nine men present in the house and three women." The inspector had done his arithmetic and put his paper away. Zoe considered, with the aid of her fingers, then nodded.

Purbright sat a little further back in his chair, looking directly at Zoe. "What I should be interested to know now," he said, "is which, among those people, might have wished you harm?"

There was a long silence.

"*Me?*"

Forgetful of elegance in her perplexity, Zoe had allowed one hand to wander and attend to an itch at the top of her thigh. Mrs. Claypole slapped it away, crossly, without taking her eyes off the inspector.

"What do you mean, harm? Nobody's done any harm. To Zoe, you mean?"

Again Purbright addressed Zoe directly. "Somebody locked you in that bathroom. I should like to know who it was."

She relaxed visibly. "Oh, that. How should I know? Somebody trying to be funny, that's all."

"You really have no idea who might have done it?"

She shrugged. "Some twit. I really wouldn't know."

Purbright turned to Mrs. Claypole. Her face blank, she stirred the contents of the teapot mechanically for some moments, then said, "Not unless it was one of that precious pair from Chalmsbury—them or their father."

Neither woman seemed to think this line worth pursuing. Zoe had finished her first cup of tea and was now eagerly watching her mother pour a second. Purbright had drunk little of his; it was very strong.

He asked if there were any appliances in the house run on bottled gas. Yes, the cooker; had he not seen the big cylinders outside the back door? He had, but was thinking of something smaller, something portable perhaps. A tubby sort of cylinder had been left, Zoe thought, in a corner of one of the rooms upstairs. The men had used it for a blowtorch when the outside painting was being done.

"Have you recently had occasion to move that gas bottle, Mrs. Loughbury?"

The question seemed to make no sense to her. Purbright rephrased it.

"Have you any idea how it came to be in a chair close to the heater in the room where the clothing caught fire today?"

This time there were two incredulous stares. The older woman found voice first.

"Do you mean to say it would have gone off? All that gas?"

"Not necessarily. But if the fire had taken hold, the risk of an explosion would have been considerable."

Mrs. Claypole looked at her daughter, then back to Purbright. "What, and her locked in . . ." Falteringly, her hand reached across for Zoe's.

CHAPTER 5

One of the harmless fictions whereby Mr. Harcourt
Chubb lightened his duties as Chief Constable of Flaxborough might be expressed in parody of Genesis: Before Monday was nothing made that was made. In
other words, the purpose and function of the Sabbath
was to shut off all that had gone before and to confer
upon the ensuing week an absolute innocence of association.

Hence it was that when Inspector Purbright attended upon him in the cool and spacious room he occupied from time to time in the Fen Street police headquarters and announced his misgivings concerning the
previous Saturday's events at Mumblesby, Mr. Chubb
gazed awhile at his cuff, then at the ceiling, and said:

"Considering that you were very kindly deputising
for me at poor Loughbury's funeral, I hardly think it
fair for you to be burdened with an investigation of
these rather questionable matters, Mr. Purbright. This
lady who purports to be the widow—I take it that she
has not made a formal complaint?"

"No, sir. I am still trying to make sense of her attitude. If someone had turned a key on me in similar circumstances I fancy I should show a little more resentment."

"Yes, but you know it is not always true that women
jump to conclusions. They sometimes take a calmer and
more cautious view than you might think—a wiser
view, indeed, than some men."

"Mrs. Loughbury is not a well-educated woman, but she is intelligent. Her wisdom I should be inclined to doubt, sir. Shrewd she is, certainly."

The chief constable spread his hands. "Well, there you are, then, Mr. Purbright. A shrewd and intelligent lady is not going to come to much harm. If she really feels threatened—and I confess I can see no reason why she should—she no doubt will let you know, having once been introduced."

Purbright's relations with Mr. Chubb, within a framework of extreme formality, were curiously confidential and allowed of a frankness that no one listening to their exchanges could have guessed. The secret lay in a code, acknowledged by neither, but developed over the years into a subtle instrument of mutual understanding.

On this Monday morning, for instance, the chief constable was left in no doubt that his detective inspector, convinced of an attempt having been made on the life of Rich Dick's concubine, intended to make himself as much of a nuisance as the law and Mr. Chubb allowed until the truth of the matter emerged. Purbright, on the other hand, was no less certainly apprised of Mr. Chubb's strong reluctance to see the reputation of a late fellow club member endangered for the sake of a girl who once had lived in a public house and now laid claim to some very nice property which she probably didn't appreciate.

Purbright climbed the ancient iron circular staircase to the floor on which was his own office. There, Sergeant Love, looking smug, joined him.

"I picked up the dope from that reporter," announced Love. He put a sheet of typescript on the desk.

"Dope?" Purbright pretended not to understand. He had tried for years to cure Love's weakness for what the sergeant fancied to be Fleet Street terminology. But then, as he always did, he felt mean and straightaway said: "Ah, *dope*—yes, I see," and picked up the list of names.

They included most, but not all, of those he had collected already himself.

"There was a bit of a do in the church, from what this chap was telling me," said Love. He related the story of Zoe's ejection of the Chalmsbury branch. Love's accounts were robbed of dramatic point, somehow, by his customary obliging, pleased-with-life expression. He would have described a public execution or a jam-making demonstration with equal cheerfulness.

Purbright told the sergeant about the fire, the locked door, the gas cylinder.

"Seems there's a rabbit away somewhere," Love commented good-naturedly. "Oh, and I was right about propane. It is the one that's bottled at higher pressure. They probably were using it to work a blowtorch."

"Why is it, do you suppose, Sid, that the young woman took it all so calmly? It was the mother who got worked up, not Zoe."

"Mothers do. Mine does."

Purbright frowned at him. He had never before considered the possibility of the sergeant's having a mother. It was enough to bear with the chronic youthfulness of his appearance without having to envisage a woman who would not be restrained from combing his hair and making sure he had a handkerchief.

"Do you know anything about Mumblesby?"

The sergeant considered. "They reckon it's a bit upper-ten-ish nowadays."

"Well off, are they?"

"So they reckon. A lot of them ride horses round

there. And it's supposed to cost eight pounds a head to eat at that café."

"Does it really?"

"We once had some trouble with a bloke who used to be the personal . . ." Love faltered. "What do they call somebody who mucks about with feet?"

"Chiropodist?"

"That's it. He used to be the Duke of Edinburgh's personal chiropodist."

"What sort of trouble?"

"Oh nothing much. He was creating in the street. Threatening somebody."

Purbright waited, but Love seemed to have emptied his store of wonders.

"So it's a village of fairly high tone," said the inspector, without guile.

"You could say so."

Purbright nodded. "In which case, we cannot send our coarser-grained ambassadors. It will have to be you, Sid. Go tomorrow. Now, listen. We can't waste a lot of time on this, but I do seriously believe that that overconfident young woman is in danger. A little well-directed eavesdropping is more likely to produce ideas of why, and from whom, than a month of heavy interrogating."

Purbright took out his record of names provided by Zoe and her mother, and set it beside the *Citizen* reporter's typescript. "Here's the nearest we have to a checklist, although we can't be sure that no one else entered the house that morning."

Love picked up both pieces of paper and carefully folded one inside the other. "Will do," he said crisply.

The expression made Purbright suddenly nervous. "Of course, this isn't a door-to-door job, Sid."

Away went the papers into Love's hip pocket; on to his face, an oh-very-droll smirk.

"Above all, don't go marching up to the Manor House as soon as you arrive. Neither she nor anyone else must get the idea that we're interested specifically in her. You'll be too near home to pretend you're not a policeman, but so long as you choose a genuine and convincing errand, you'll be all right."

The natural roseate glow of Love's complexion intensified. "I could talk to the servants, if you like—you know, get their confidence."

Purbright stared, then swallowed. "Yes, do that, Sid. Talk to the servants by all means."

The House of Yesteryear, in Northgate, Flaxborough, once had been a corn chandler's. A smell of grain bins lingered still, not unpleasantly, in the two adjoining showrooms where Miss Teatime's stock-in-trade was set out.

When Inspector Purbright entered, he saw Miss Teatime at the further end, in conversation with a man and woman. They were interested, it seemed, in quite the largest item in the shop: a quarter acre or so of dried spinach, flecked with fragments of orange peel, massively framed and entitled "Before Sebastopol." Hearing the opening of the door, she turned her head and smiled acknowledgement. Purbright hoped the couple would not take too long to realise that the picture was not a portable exhibit but virtually a fourth wall. He started to pass the time by looking at what he presumed was a butter churn.

Miss Teatime did not keep him long.

"My dear Inspector, how encouraging to find that the appurtenances of quieter times can lure you from the battle against crime, even for a little while."

"I thought you might put me in the way of a nice secondhand treadmill, actually." He gave the hand she offered him a squeeze of genuine affability.

Miss Teatime said she could do him some gyves. She indicated an abstract in rust. Its only identifiable feature was the appended ticket marked £32.

"Do you know," she said with sudden earnestness, "that it is extremely difficult to come by decent examples of manacles. They are extremely collectable, of course; eighteenth century especially. What people will pay highly for are the attested models."

"Autographed?"

"Inspector, you are not being serious. When I tell you that the handcuffs used on Crippen, certificated by Dew, would fetch at least twenty thousand pounds at auction, you will realise I am not joking."

Purbright said he would see what he could do for her. In the meantime, it was her expertise in quite another field that he hoped he might tap.

She would be delighted. Where did his interest lie?

"Sacred relics."

The small, still rather pretty, nose wrinkled. "Oh, dear—not *ikons?*"

"No, not ikons."

"You are wise. Most of them are quite spurious, you know. A friend of mine in Lon . . . no, that is to say, someone in the trade, of whom I have been warned, is reputed to mass-produce the things in glass beads and poster paint."

"Good heavens," said Purbright. Then, "No, I am thinking of a much more fundamental area. Fragments of the True Cross, no less."

Miss Teatime arched her finely delineated brows. "Not, I am happy to say, Inspector, an English-based industry. One would employ a Byzantine agent, I should say. Would you like me to make inquiries for you?"

Purbright said he thought not. "Let me put my problem in this way," he said. "Suppose I had come across

a collector—a well-informed and intelligent collector—
who had acquired an article represented to be a piece
of the Golgotha cross, and he had gone to considerable trouble and expense not only to safeguard it but
actually to display the thing, what should I think about
him?"

Miss Teatime regarded the inspector for several
seconds. "The question, of course, is rhetorical?"

"I should appreciate an answer, nevertheless."

"Very well. The man clearly is potty."

"As it happens," Purbright said, "he is dead."

Miss Teatime smiled to herself, and rearranged a se-
lection of Georgian toothpicks. "Now we are getting
somewhere," she remarked, softly.

"Have you made the acquaintance of the young
woman who lives in the Manor House at Mumblesby?"
Purbright asked.

Miss Teatime said she had met Mrs. Loughbury on
the day before her husband's funeral. "My colleague,
Mr. Harrington, manages our little gallery in the village. We felt it would be appropriate to call and pay
our respects."

"I believe she calls herself Mrs. Claypole-Loughbury."

"Ah, does she? A singularly perspicacious young
woman. With that name, and that address, she could
get tick anywhere in London."

"If she proves to be the beneficiary of Richard
Loughbury, I doubt if she will need it."

Miss Teatime sighed.

"Have you," Purbright asked her, "seen anything of
the contents of the house? I did wonder, in view of
your professional interests."

"I have not made an inventory, if that is what you
mean."

"Perish the thought."

"But within the limits of courtesy and grief, I did manage to spy out some very nice stuff—the value of which, I hasten to add, the young woman seems fully to realise." Miss Teatime paused. "I did not notice any holy relics."

"No, you wouldn't—unless you went upstairs."

She regarded him sharply. "In a bedroom?"

"Yes . . . well, a dressing room, I suppose one would call it."

"That is interesting. As you will know better than I, the owner of valuable objects will often cherish the notion that his prize possession is safer for being physically close, particularly at night. An extreme example is the person who hides things under the mattress."

Purbright said he had heard of the practice.

Miss Teatime laughed. "I must sound like a burglar alarm salesman. No, the point is that if—as one would naturally suppose—Mr. Loughbury had bought this so-called relic in order to amuse his friends, he would have displayed it prominently in his drawing room. His keeping it upstairs suggests he really did put a very high price on the thing. I did not know the gentleman; had he a streak of simplemindedness?"

"On the contrary, he was generally considered to be devious."

She shook her head. "In that case, Mr. Purbright, it would appear that he was an eccentric as well. I can assure you that traffickers in saints' kneecaps are no longer in the big money."

They moved further into the shop. Purbright paused to examine a silver lemon squeezer. It was tagged £130. He replaced it without remark, watched by Miss Teatime.

"You are thinking to yourself that the price is exorbitant."

He pouted. "Steep-ish."

"Provenance is all," she said. "That was Oscar Wilde's private lemon squeezer. It was kept in the kitchens of the Café Royale until just after the First World War."

"My Mr. Love—whom I think you know"—Miss Teatime said yes, of course she knew the sergeant—"has a personal tankard reserved for him in the Roebuck Tap. I think it makes him feel like François Villon."

Miss Teatime released as near a giggle as her customary niceness of behaviour allowed.

They passed on. Miss Teatime pointed to a small rectangular tin with a picture upon it of a man in the uniform of the Grenadier Guards, benevolently distributing Huntley & Palmer's biscuits to a medley of half-size black, brown and yellow men, all somehow enveloped in a Union Jack.

"Provenance again," she said. "On the face of it, just a biscuit tin: one of several hundred distributed to the schoolchildren of Flaxborough on Empire Day, 1907." She handed it to Purbright. "But look underneath."

He saw initials childishly scratched through the varnish. Miss Teatime's delicate pink forefinger delineated the letters. "T . . . E . . . L . . . you see? L for Lawrence, of course."

"Of Arabia?" Purbright reverently turned the tin about until he could see the price ticket.

"The very same. Few people, I imagine," said Miss Teatime, taking the tin back and replacing it, "can be aware that Lawrence of Arabia attended Spindle Lane Infants' School, here in Flaxborough." She glanced at Purbright's face, then away again. "For a short time," she added.

Purbright picked up what appeared to be a pair of scissors with a small blue glass jar dependent from one blade. Miss Teatime told him that she would not identify the article because she had no wish to strain his credence, but its use was indelicate and the price correspondingly low at twenty-eight pounds.

He said he did not know how she managed to live.

They strolled towards an outcrop of pine furniture that appeared to have been assembled by mad axemen and priced by mad accountants.

A sidelong glance at her face told Purbright that Miss Teatime, looking pensive now, was nearing the moment when she would, with no sign either of concern or condescension, present him with some piece of relevant and perhaps even vital information. They looked at the pine for a few moments, then at a small but choice collection of road-repair lanterns.

"Reverting," said Miss Teatime, "to the general subject of provenance . . ."

"Yes?"

"And to the more particular subject of Mr. Loughbury's belongings . . ."

Purbright waited in silence.

". . . my own brief observation and limited inquiries have produced some rather interesting results. I regret that relics do not enter into the matter, but a number of genuinely valuable objects certainly do.

"I am speaking of various paintings, one or two small pieces of sculpture, some silver, candlesticks, snuffboxes and so on—all of which are to be seen in the big drawing room at the house. You may well have noticed them yourself."

Purbright said that he had, but without paying particular attention to them.

"Of course," resumed Miss Teatime, "when I said that I made no inventory of what I saw, it was not to suggest that I ignored it. Once Mr. Harrington and I had withdrawn from the house of mourning, we compared observations and noted down a number of articles—for professional reference.

"Over the weekend, with the aid of various colleagues in the trade, we did a little research."

"Into provenance?" prompted Purbright.

Miss Teatime beamed, then became solemn again.

"Now, the odd thing is this: in the case of nearly all the choicest articles, the last traceable owner was not merely someone in the same general area—that might not seem unreasonable—but an actual inhabitant of the same little village."

"And that does seem unreasonable?"

"When things of this nature change hands, Mr. Purbright, one does not expect the sale to be a casual deal between neighbours. Experts are involved, usually, and even if auction procedure is not employed, the details are recorded. Mr. Loughbury was a solicitor: he, of all people, might be expected to have been meticulous in such matters."

"Is it your suggestion that the man's title to these things is questionable?"

"I certainly do not suggest that he pinched them. Not in a policeman's sense of the word."

"In whose, then?"

Both smiled.

"Let me give you an illustration, Inspector. There is hanging now in Mumblesby Manor House a picture called 'Staircase with Valves' by Paul Klee. It is worth a great deal of money. Art dealers, who make it their business to know the whereabouts of such things, believe it still to be in the possession of the gentleman who was left it in a relative's will about twenty years ago—a Mr. Robin Cork-Bradden."

"Of Mumblesby."

"Precisely."

"Is there no record—within the trade, as I think you would put it—of the transfer of the picture to Mr. Loughbury?"

"None—and Mr. Harrington has extremely reliable

sources of information. If money passed, the transaction was kept extraordinarily secret."

"Could not the painting have been a gift?" Purbright asked.

She smiled. "Upwards of fifteen thousand pounds' worth of gift?" A little later: "One or two other items from Mr. Cork-Bradden's collection appear also to have found their way to the Manor House without anyone's noticing. Some quite outstandingly fine Bristol glass, for instance. I do hope that the bereaved lady will not wash it up with the tea things."

"You could offer to relieve her of the responsibility."

"Not, I fear, at present market prices."

"Did Mr. Loughbury acquire things from any other close neighbours?"

"So it would seem. The candlesticks, for instance—a most unusual pair in silver gilt, French, early seventeenth century—belonged to a Mr. Bishop. He lives in that lovely Georgian house in Church Lane. Mr. Harrington remembers seeing the candlesticks there when he first came to the village."

The tinkling of a little bell and the sound of the street door being pushed open signalled a fresh customer. Miss Teatime prepared to receive ("serve" was scarcely the word in the context of *fin de siècle* lemon squeezers) the new arrival.

Purbright thanked her and they moved together towards the door. On the way, he indicated with a nod the initialled biscuit tin.

"Rather a backward boy," he remarked.

"Backward?"

"Yes, Lawrence of Arabia. Still attending Infants' School in 1907. He would have been nineteen."

There was only the briefest of pauses. Miss Teatime laughed.

"No, no, Inspector—*evening* classes. In navigation, I think it was."

CHAPTER 6

Although Detective Sergeant Sidney Love had an aunt living in a remote country area near Strawbridge, whom he fondly visited from time to time, he was an urban dweller by upbringing and by preference, and retained many of the townsman's ideas about rural life.

Upon his arrival in Mumblesby at eleven o'clock on Tuesday morning, he made his way immediately towards the village inn, confident that beyond a door marked BAR PARLOUR or even SNUG, there awaited him in bucolic carouse as many of the local peasantry as could be spared from harvest field, stables and kitchen.

The Barleybird, formerly the Red Lion, had been built in the eighteenth century as a coaching inn, but there came no coaches now, nor even buses. Behind the tall windows in the high, handsome stone frontage were rooms mostly empty. A barrier had been set across the arched entrance to the yard, for latter-day customers in motorcars, while lacking nothing of the élan of the coachman atop the old Lincoln Flyer, were a good deal less skilful at negotiating the passage. There was, in any case, plenty of parking space on two sides of the marketplace, where no market had been held since Victorian times.

Love found the present-day entrance to the Barleybird was a porched door at the side of the building. It led to a lobby, carpeted in deep green and smelling of lavatory deodorant. On his left was a little office with a sliding glass window. No one was in the office.

Two doors marked PRIVATE were on his right, a pair of glass doors immediately in front of him. No intimation so far of snug, nor yet bar parlour. Love looked through the glass. He saw a big undivided room, with a bar running its whole length. The woman behind the bar looked up from rinsing a glass. She had a black dress and yellowish hair.

It was clear that Love had chosen the wrong day to meet Mumblesby's retainers and body servants. The only other customer in the bar was a woman of sixty or so, with white, wiry hair that contrasted strikingly with the deeply tanned, leathery skin of her narrow, alert face. She was wearing a shabby tweed jacket and a pair of voluminous, chocolate-coloured slacks. A silk Paisley scarf was tied close to her throat. As she sat cross-legged on a tall bar-side chair, she held a cigarette between long, bony finger and thumb and examined it with fierce concentration.

The sergeant said "Good morning" in a commendatory and very cheerful way, as if he had come to sell something.

The woman behind the bar had finished rinsing the glass and was now screwing a towel into it. She trained a sad eye upon Love and gave her head a little upward toss which opened her mouth at the same time.

"A pint of your best bitter," declared Love, who knew about robust country ways.

The woman looked about her, searched for a moment beneath the bar counter, and retreated through a door at her back. When she reappeared, she was carrying a pint glass, which she held to the light and rubbed round the rim with a middle finger before filling it with beer, which she did by twice pouring the contents of a half-pint glass into it.

"Oh, Sadie, for heaven's *sake!*"

It was the white-haired woman. She had been

watching the performance with a thin, mocking smile. Now she turned to Love.

"The dear, *dear* girl *al*ways but *al*ways goes through this . . ."—she flapped a hand weakly—". . . this *thing* with *beer*. But you mustn't take any *no*tice. Sadie's really *rather* a *dar*ling."

The sergeant guessed at once that here was gentry, if not actual aristocracy. He gave the woman a grin, then offered another, much smaller, to Sadie, who had gone back to screwing her towel into glasses.

"Connie Whybrow," announced the woman, without italics this time. Her face was assertively uptilted, friendly.

Lucky me, Love told himself. A listed person at first shot.

"Pleased to meet you." He did not volunteer his identity. She would ask him, though. Funny thing, the upper ten were not polite.

She looked him up and down and glanced at his pint. "Insurance, Mr. . . . ?"

He shook his head promptly and cheerily. "The name's Love, actually."

"*Good God!*"

"Sidney Love," he added, hastily. He had expected a little upper-class banter, but Mrs. Whybrow's habit of heavy syllabic emphasis was most disconcerting.

"Love . . . *Sid*ney Love . . . *Sid*ney *Love* . . ." Musingly she repeated the words. "But how *ab*solutely too sweet." She reached suddenly and captured his forearm, which she gently pulled to and fro whilst addressing the barmaid:

"Sadie, did you *hear?* Did you *hear* the gentleman's *name?* Now you *must* open a bottle of champagne or give us *all* drinks on the *house* or just simply ca*vort* or something."

Sadie responded by moving to the other end of the

bar, where she began to refill the roasted-peanut dispenser.

"But you *should* be in insurance," Mrs. Whybrow asserted. "I mean, round *here* you'd just take people's money for *ever*. I mean nobody ever *dies*, so you wouldn't have to pay *out*, would you?"

Love said he supposed not.

Mrs. Whybrow, who had released his arm once, now seized it again.

"Never mind," she said. "With such an absolutely *marv*ellous name, I'm sure you *must* do something quite *wild*ly exciting, and I think the village ought to be *thrilled* about it."

Love swallowed. "I'm a policeman, as a matter of fact, Mrs. Whybrow."

As he told Purbright afterwards, the words had come out of their own accord, like a cry for help. "You blew your cover, Sid," Purbright was to tell him, but only in fun.

The strong, bony hand tightened its grip. "A po*lice*-man!" The voice, dry with smoking and gin, had become suddenly hard as a man's. But then it trilled away huskily once more: an echo from some Claridge's party in the thirties.

"Oh, but that's *much* too good to be true. I'm sorry, but I simply *don't* believe you, Mr. Cupid. You don't look in the *least* like a policeman."

Which happened to be true. Love tried to scowl. He muttered, "Detective sergeant," and took a gulp of his drink.

"*Do* tell me," said Mrs. Whybrow, with furtive leer, "what you've come to in*vest*igate. Is it something terribly . . ." The adjective eluding her, she flapped the hand that seemed to serve as a subsidiary vocabulary.

Love used the opportunity to move and sit down just beyond danger of further arrest.

"Routine," he said airily. "Stolen property. Missing persons. We get these lists. I mean, there's no one here *act*ually *sus*pected." Exposure to Mrs. Whybrow's verbal idiosyncrasy clearly carried risk of infection.

"My dear *sweet*, I cannot bring myself to believe *that*. This village is absolutely *swarming* with suspicious characters. They come *in*, you know."

"Foreigners?" Love knew country-dwellers liked quaint terms.

"Oh, no—*English*," insisted Mrs. Whybrow, who had been born and bred in South London. "That makes it worse . . . or am I being old-fashioned and *tiresome?*"

"Not a bit, madam," Love assured her. The "madam" brought a cracked whoop of delight from Mrs. Whybrow. She chain-lit another cigarette and ground the discarded stub into an ashtray as if into the face of an enemy.

Love wondered if this would be a good moment to begin the establishment of confidence. He glanced at the small quantity of colourless liquid in Mrs. Whybrow's glass. It looked like something pretty expensive. Better not rush things.

"Sad about Mr. Loughbury," he said.

Mrs. Whybrow stared at him. "What do you mean, *sad?*" One eye was screwed shut to escape the thin blue fume from the cigarette; the other glared in disbelief.

Love shrugged and blew out his cheeks a little.

"Sa . . a . . ad?" bleated Mrs. Whybrow with terrible irony.

Again Love gave a little lift to his shoulders. "Not nice. Dying . . ." He pouted and regarded one shoe in a melancholy fashion.

At that moment, Love heard someone enter the room and walk heavily to the bar. Mrs. Whybrow grinned past him at the new arrival.

"Morning, Win."

Love heard a grunt, then the rattle of coins on wood. Guardedly, he turned his head.

The man he saw, shortsightedly raking amongst the money he had unloaded on the bar top from the pocket of his huge clay-coloured windcheater, was of a size that had to be assessed by instalments. His feet, each a furrow broad, were encased in Wellingtons that would have kennelled a brace of bull terriers. His thighs might have defied comparison with articles of husbandry smaller than long-back porkers, save that they were so proportionately diminished by the belly overhanging them that they actually looked frail. That central, commanding belly-mass detracted, too, from the man's chest, but it was a big chest for all that, a barn of a chest. One arm hung inert by his side, the gammon-sized hand a few inches from the floor. With the other he shovelled coins forward in negligent prodigality.

The barmaid drifted down-bar. Without consultation, she drew two shots of Haig into a glass and put it before the big man. He left her to take what money she wanted and straightaway swallowed some of the whiskey.

Love marvelled at the man's headpiece. It was round, narrowing at the top, where thin, unnoticeable hair was stranded. In the long ears was more hair, stiffer this, and gingery. The eyes, watchful and evasive by turns, were so pale by contrast with the puce cheeks, nose and neck, as to suggest their having been blanched by the protection of his close, gold-rimmed glasses, in the manner of salad legumes in a forcing frame.

"Winnie, you *must* meet my nice friend," declared Mrs. Whybrow over Love's head. Love moved his chair through ninety degrees and donned a conciliatory expression. The big man gave no sign of having heard anything.

Undeterred, Mrs. Whybrow conducted introductions.

"This is Mr. Sidney *Love*—I wanted to call him *Cupid*, of course, but that would be against the *law* or something, so we'd better not—anyway, Love's rather sweet, don't you think—and this" (Love got his hand ready) "is Mr. Winston Gash, who farms an absolutely *fab*ulous number of *acres,* or whatever people do farm, and is *dread*fully rich."

Love declared himself pleased to make Mr. Gash's acquaintance.

Mr. Gash vouchsafed the slightest of nods and turned from the rashly offered hand to address the lady behind the bar.

"Now, then, dimple-tits."

Sadie gave sign of neither offence nor pleasure.

"Mr. Love and I were *just* talking," Mrs. Whybrow said to the farmer's vast back, "about *poor* Mr. Loughbury's upping and *dying* so *ridiculously* suddenly."

Sounds emerged from the further side of the farmer's bulk. "O-ar?"

"Of course, Mr. Loughbury *rode*, you know," Mrs. Whybrow told Love, as if warning him to take the matter seriously.

Mr. Gash's back heaved. He said something to Sadie which caused her to look away sourly.

"He *rode*," Mrs. Whybrow repeated, "with the *Ham*bourne, actually."

"Going to let me have a feel, then?" Mr. Gash inquired of Sadie, then, without turning round: "Want a gin, do you, Connie?"

Mrs. Whybrow's glass was on the counter, empty, almost before Love was aware of movement. She signalled him to join in taking advantage of the benefaction while it was going.

Love dispatched the rest of his beer as quickly as he could but without enjoyment, and set the glass beside Mrs. Whybrow's. Mr. Gash, who still had not varied his position of leaning slightly inward, four-square to the bar, fingered his own glass forward, then Mrs. Whybrow's. Sadie refilled both and selected some coins from the farmer's bar-top exchequer. Finally, she picked up Love's pint glass and looked at him in mute inquiry. He shrugged. Sadie filled it with beer. Love paid.

After a short silence, the voice of farmer Gash was heard once more.

"Git any last night, then?"

His habit of speaking without the slightest change of posture made it difficult to determine who was being addressed. Love thought it was most probably Sadie. He was also thinking that, unpromising as the conversation was, it was not likely to reach a more useful level unless he did some prompting.

"I suppose," he said, rather loudly, "that there's a lot of sympathy in the village for Mrs. Loughbury?"

There was a very long pause, then "Wotsy say?" Mr. Gash inquired of no one in particular.

Mrs. Whybrow donned a pained smile. "I take it you mean Miss *Clay*pole. The sort of *house*keeper or whatever."

"I mean the lady in occupation of the Manor House," Love said, policemanishly. He added: "Known as Mrs. Zoe Claypole-Loughbury."

Mr. Gash's shoulders jerked; a short word, deplorably recognisable, emerged from behind them.

"Strictly entre *nous*," Mrs. Whybrow said to Love, "we are not madly ap*prov*ing of our Zoe."

"Why is that, madam?" The sergeant's face was a

picture of innocent curiosity. Mrs. Whybrow regarded it for several moments as if in doubt of its reality.

"*Why?* My dear boy, what do you mean, *why?* God knows I'm not a snob, but the woman's a *parvenu.* Have you *met* her? A *pea*sant, I promise you. She really is."

A sudden recollection sharpened Mrs. Whybrow's manner. She leaned closer. "You said you were looking for stolen property . . ."

"Just routine inquiries," said Love, hastily.

Someone was entering the bar at the far end. Mrs Whybrow lowered her voice; it became a growl. "No names, no pack-drill, dear boy, but some *wickedly* costly stuff has found its way into the same house as La Claypole. All very *odd.*"

The new arrival had been joined by two others. All were men. They remained close to the door, talking; one held the door a little open, as for a companion slightly delayed.

"It really is *dread*ful of me to be talking to you like this," whispered Mrs. Whybrow with a new and considerable eagerness, "but it does so happen that two of the gentlemen who've just come in . . ."

"Gin, Connie?"

With a speed and agility of which Love would not dream him capable, Winston Gash had turned about and was lowering over Mrs. Whybrow like a building about to collapse. She grinned at him and handed over her glass.

Two of the new arrivals were now approaching. The larger, Love recognised. It was Spencer Gash, farming brother of Winston. The others addressed him as Spen.

With Spencer's companion, a man of about her own age but lacking her appearance of healthy preservation, Mrs. Whybrow seemed to be on terms too familiar to call for greeting. Love surmised that here was

Mr. Raymond Bishop, Mrs. Whybrow's lodger in Church Lane.

Mrs. Whybrow nudged the sergeant and spoke low. "Mr. Bishop is, as they say, my paying guest—except that he doesn't pay—no, no, no, that's just my little joke —he really is the most *fear*fully nice old chap, and I don't care, quite *frankly*, if he pays or not. If there were any justice in this world, dear Raymond would be a Companion of *Honour* or something, but the whole thing's most *aw*fully sad . . . Oh, God, Winnie, but how *fiend*ishly kind of you . . ."

Winston Gash had thrust upon her a brimming glass. Some spirit slopped down her thigh, leaving a dark trail on the brown trouser leg. Love immediately handed her his spare, unblown-upon handkerchief, kept for good causes. "What a *sweetie* you are!" declared Mrs. Whybrow, and he blushed. "Peed yoursen?" inquired Mr. Gash.

Mrs. Whybrow applied Love's handkerchief energetically to the gin streaks. "One thing you *must* be careful of," she said between rubs. "However familiarly Mr. Bishop may address you, *please* do *not* call him Ray. It would upset him absolutely *dread*fully."

Love said he would remember.

Mrs. Whybrow nodded and put Love's handkerchief in her handbag.

"When you've been something ter*rific*ally important, like a *surgeon* or whatever," she said, "it simply isn't *bearable* to be talked to as if you're a *plumber* or a *bank* clerk . . . I mean, Mr. Bishop used to be . . ." She stopped, shook her head very decidedly, and tapped the ash from her cigarette onto Love's knee. "No, you mustn't ask me—it's too *terribly* top secret."

She looked up, brightening, at the person under discussion, and said, as sweetly as to a child: "Isn't it, darling? Simply *too* secret for words?"

Whatever things Mr. Bishop had been in the past, tall must have been one of them. Now he stooped, as if set by long years of condescension. The stoop robbed him, as it were, of his neck, and made of his rounded shoulders, head, brow, macaw-like nose and receding chin, one continuous curve, a huge comma. Tucked into the corner of the comma was an affable, rather dreamy smile.

"Pleased to meet you, Mr. Bishop," said Love, reading the smile as readiness to be friendly.

Bishop turned to Mrs. Whybrow and weakly jabbed a finger in Love's direction.

"Who's that?"

"It's Mr. Love, darling."

"Don't be ridiculous." Mr. Bishop smiled on, but the finger movement now was dismissive.

"I am *not* being ridiculous, sweetheart. Mr. Love and I are good friends." She grabbed the sergeant's hand and grinned at him, showing all her teeth.

"I don't want anything in the newspapers. The chap understands, does he? Nothing in the papers, tell him."

Love, as he was to explain to Purbright, had come to the conclusion by now that the Barleybird Inn was the resort not of talkative menials but of that particular section of the upper class that delights in the discomfiture of police officers. He stared at Bishop with cherubic concern and asked firmly: "What is it that you wish to be kept out of the newspapers, sir?"

The ensuing silence told the sergeant that he had won a wider audience than he had intended.

The gravelly voice of Mrs. Whybrow was first to be heard again.

"But *Ray*mond, darling, the gentleman isn't a *reporter* or anything dreadful like *that*. As far as anything's ever clear to poor little *me*, I gather he's come to the village to look for lost *prop*erty. He's a sort of detective."

"Special Branch, is he?" Mr. Bishop appeared to find this possibility very much to his taste, but still not attractive enough to entitle Love to direct address.

"I am not from the Special Branch, sir, but if you wish to confide in one of their officers, I feel sure that arrangements could be made!"

Someone had handed Mr. Bishop a drink. He paid it prompt and concentrated attention, leaning forward to the glass while his elbow jutted out like a boxer's guard. When he had finished, he handed the empty glass to Mrs. Whybrow, who put it on the bar. She seemed used to doing him these small services.

"Tell him not to bother me about it, Booboo, will you? If the Special Branch require my services, they'll be in touch, I doubt not."

Another drink was coming Mr. Bishop's way, borne by Spencer Gash. Love reflected that there was a fair old turnover of larrup in Mumblesby on a weekday morning. He covertly surveyed Spen and other new arrivals.

Farmer Spencer was not so bulky a man as his brother, but had a powerful build, set off by hacking jacket and fawn cavalry twill trousers of better quality than the occasion would have seemed to warrant. His head was narrow, his nose long and lean, and the moustache traversing the full line of his upper lip had been shaved in a meticulously straight line. He wore a formal shirt and tie and a foxhead tiepin in gold enamel. His voice was high, a little adenoidal. The drink he ordered for himself was a strong bottled lager with brandy chaser. Mr. Gash Mark II addressed no word of impropriety to the woman behind the bar, but his look lingered long after each unexceptionable remark. The look, Sadie once had told a friend, was like hot gravy spilling slowly down the front of her dress.

By now, Mrs. Whybrow was ready with more introductions.

One was to a man in his sixties. Curly grey hair, much receded, a face taking on fleshiness despite a determinedly energetic expression, good suit, immediate attentiveness. Love knew him. At one time head of a Flaxborough canning firm, he was the latter-day proprietor of the Old Mill Restaurant.

"Leonard, dearest boy, you must meet my *amorous* policeman—Love—amorous— No? Oh, *dear*, perhaps rather *not* . . . anyway, Mr. Love, this *luscious* gentleman is Mr. *Pal*grove, and he and his charming wife serve the *most* wonderful food."

"How do you do, Mr. Palgrove," said Love.

A large hand, white but with black hairs at the wrist, shot forward. "Len," commanded its owner.

Love offered a weak smile of recognition, but it was not enough. His own hand was seized and held hostage while Mr. Palgrove peered closely into his face.

"It's Sidney, isn't it? Lovely to see you again."

Palgrove turned away, looking for other important engagements.

Mr. Bishop giggled.

From the direction of Winston Gash: "Hey, when diddy last gittis legovver?"

Mrs. Whybrow smirked. "I rather *think* he means *you*," she confided to Love.

The sergeant was frowning. "Who does?"

"Winnie—the big gentleman facing the bar."

"Why should he mean me?"

"It's a question he puts to everybody, actually. He really is quite *sweet*. You mustn't mind. Being asked that is a sort of compliment round here."

"Hey. That copper. Babbychops. Ar reckon 'e's nivver addis legovver."

"I don't think that's supposed to be a compliment," Love observed to Mrs. Whybrow.

"Never mind, here's an *ab*solutely *per*fect gentleman for you. He be able to talk about stolen property for *ab*solutely *hours*. Who better, poor darling? Robin— come and have *colloquy*, or whatever one has on these occasions, with this *fearfully* understanding policeman."

Whatever the expectations of Mrs. Whybrow, who, at this stage, temporarily quit the bar, Mr. Robin Cork-Bradden made it plain to Sergeant Love that he knew of nothing of value ever having been stolen from his premises or wrested from his possession by force or guile. He then courteously excused himself.

By the time Mrs. Whybrow returned, she seemed to have forgotten the sergeant. The hoots and brays of her conversation rose from within a group that had formed near the fireplace. No one else showed sign of wanting to adopt her late protégé. He certainly was in no danger of being bought more beer. That did not distress him. The only beverage of which he could be said to be fond was raisin wine.

Love sat on in his isolation, listening to what he could make out of the conversation. Mr. Bishop was telling Mr. Cork-Bradden about protocol at Marlborough House. Mr. Palgrove enthused to Farmer Spencer Gash on the subject of his "old girl"—not, it seemed, his wife, but an Aston Martin motorcar. Spencer rejoindered whenever he was able with references to his own favoured means of transport, which he called "the Murk." Horses were being discussed by two younger men with pale eyes and hair cut in a very straight line at the nape; their lady companions wore headscarves and very dirty, narrow-legged trousers, and flicked the ash off their cigarettes every time they said, "Oh, *God*, yes," which was fairly often. Another farmer—short, fat and with a salami-like complexion—had docked with Winston Gash at the bar and both now were exploring the subject of "gittin' legs ovver" with sidelong references to every woman in the company in turn.

Love decided reluctantly that the Barleybird had not been a good idea. He began making his way, as unobtrusively as he could, towards the swing doors.

Some twenty people now were present. None took the slightest notice of his departure, save Mrs. Whybrow, who, on catching sight of him, shut her eyes tight and displayed her front teeth as if kneed in the groin: it was her version of a farewell smile. Before slipping through the doors, he looked back, meaning to nod a good-bye to the woman behind the bar. He couldn't see her.

In the lobby he heard a quick step behind him.

"Mister . . ." He turned.

Sadie, rather out of breath, had entered the lobby by another door.

"I just slipped out for a second. That lot won't tell you anything. Were you asking about Detty?"

"Betty?"

"No, Detty. Bernadette. Mrs. Croll."

Perplexity lent Love a slightly comic expression. The woman looked disappointed, embarrassed.

"I'm sorry, I thought . . ." She turned.

"No, don't go. Why did you think I was asking questions about Mrs. Croll?"

The woman paused, her hand on the doorknob. Swaying slightly, she stared at her own hand as it caressed and leaned upon the knob by turns.

Her voice was an anxious murmur. "They aren't on

about my little old boy again, are they? About taking him away?"

Voices. Somebody was coming down the stairs. Quickly, Sadie tugged open the door and was gone.

CHAPTER 7

Detective Sergeant Love having decided that half a day in Mumblesby was enough to manage in one go, he presented himself in Purbright's office soon after lunch.

"I expect," he said, "that you'll want a debriefing session."

He saw Purbright's stare of innocent bewilderment.

"You'll want to know how I got on in Mumblesby."

"Ah." The inspector looked relieved. "Yes, Sid, of course."

Love had made some notes, which now he assembled on his knee. He looked up.

"They're a very queer bunch."

"So I believe," said Purbright. He had been making some notes himself. They were pinned to the list of mourners at Richard Loughbury's funeral.

"There's an old cove who calls his landlady Booboo," said Love. He added: "That's for starters."

Purbright glanced down his names. "Would that, by any chance, be Mr. Bishop?"

Love nodded, then considered. "I'm not sure now that he is a chiropodist. His landlady mentioned surgeons. I think the Royal Family bit is right, though."

The inspector glanced up, one eyebrow raised. With undiminished blandness, Love added: "It didn't shake him when I offered to put him in touch with the Special Branch."

"Where did this conversation take place, Sid?"

"In that pub they call the Barleybird. People talk in

pubs. And they're not suspicious—not as they would be at home."

"Not even when invited to assignations with the Special Branch?"

Love said: "The trouble is, it's hard to get people like that to talk about what *you* want them to talk about—if you see what I mean."

"I do, indeed."

"That Mrs. Whybrow would go on all day and night, but only when it's something that *she's* interested in. I'll say this for her, she's not easily shocked."

Purbright said he hoped Love had not been indelicate in his approach.

"Oh, no, it's the farmers. They don't seem to care what they say in front of women."

"That," said the inspector, "is because they don't keep stock anymore. The purely arable farmer is no longer in the habit of restraining his language for the sake of the milk yield. Cows used to have a civilising influence on farmers."

The sergeant glanced through his notes quickly once more in search of such instances of modest success as they contained.

"Point one," he announced. "There's not much grief in Mumblesby over Rich Dick's death. Well, not among the drinking set anyway. They seemed quite offhand about it."

Purbright waited.

"Point two. They don't think much of his widow, if that's what she is. Mrs. Whybrow called her"—and the sergeant made close reference to his note—"La Claypole. Almost as if she was foreign."

"Any other comments?"

"One of the farmers—Mr. Winston Gash—used a very offensive word, but I don't think that means much, coming from him. Incidentally, I noticed something interesting about Gash. I'll tell you what it was in a minute. Point three first, though."

Love put a tick against one of his items.

"Stolen property," he went on, "is what I gave out that I was looking into."

The inspector recognised in this extreme case of ruptured syntax a sign that Love was preparing a revelation.

"Nobody gave actual instances, mind," said Love, "but Mrs. Whybrow said that there's no end of stuff at old Loughbury's place that doesn't belong there. And she was hinting like mad that two of those who'd been done were the Cork-Bradden character and an old friend of ours." He paused. "Guess who."

"I really have no idea, Sid. Tell me."

"Pally Palgrove," announced Love, with a touch of pride. "He keeps that café—the eight-pounds-a-head one."

"I should not have supposed," said Purbright, "that Mr. Palgrove was either wealthy enough or of sufficiently good taste to amass much worth stealing."

"He married into money second time round—or so Bill Malley says."

Purbright conceded the point; Sergeant Malley, the coroner's officer, was the nearest thing to an infallible oracle that Flaxborough possessed.

"She was Cynthia Barraclough, wife of that hotel manager out at Brocklestone."

"Ah, yes," murmured Purbright, comfortably. It was pleasant when names dropped into place, like cards in a promising game of patience.

"Used to be a Wilson," Love added. "It'll be her money and what she got after the divorce that set them up. And she'll have learned the catering side at her first husband's place."

"The Neptune."

"That's right."

Love recalled something. "I was going to tell you what I noticed about Gash—the big one, Winston. He'd been ignoring me and pretty well everyone else, but as soon as Mrs. Whybrow started talking about people in the village who'd lost things, there he was—standing over her. To buy her a drink, or so he said. But she kept off the subject from then on."

"Do you think he was threatening her?"

"In a way, yes. She's not the sort of lady who'd change the subject first to be obliging."

"Was she frightened?"

"Oh, no." Love appeared to find the notion amusing.

Purbright had in his hand a pencil with which he gently tapped his lower lip from time to time. Now he held the pencil before him, like an artist sizing up proportions, and regarded its sharpened end dreamily.

"Tell me, Sid—before the general subject of stolen property was dropped, was there any mention by anybody of holy relics?"

"What you were on about before, you mean."

Purbright saw that the question was a nonstarter. (Love's only brush with the occult had been his purchase, while on holiday in Cornwall with his young lady, of a Lucky Pixie charm, which he had worn under his vest until his contraction of unlucky dermatitis a fortnight later.) He shook his head and said, "Never mind."

"Point five," declared the sergeant.

And he told of his encounter with Sadie in the Barleybird lobby.

Purbright heard him out with reviving interest.

"Bernadette Croll," the inspector said, dreamily. "Good lord." Then, "Why on earth should the woman have supposed you were interested in Mrs. Croll?"

"I didn't get a chance to ask her."

"Was she mentioned by anyone else you saw this morning?"

Love shook his head. "Only by Sadie. It's Sadie Howell, by the way. Miss."

"I expect Croll still farms at Mumblesby, does he?"

"Ben? Yes, he's still there."

"Not remarried?"

"No."

"No. I suppose Bernadette would take some following."

Love looked pleased, then prim. "She had a terrible reputation."

"Not at the inquest, she didn't. The talk was all of religious mania, not nympho."

"You weren't here," Love said, a little defensively. "You were on holiday. Superintendent Larch came over from Chalmsbury."

"Yes," said Purbright. "He did, and I was. But I did read the depositions afterwards."

"Mr. Larch," said Love, "wasn't very keen on standing in for other people."

"Understandable," said Purbright.

"I remember him trying to push Bill Malley around."

"Now, Sid, the superintendent was always a most conscientious officer."

"Bill let him get on with it," said the sergeant, carelessly.

"Of course. So?"

Love shrugged. "Nothing."

"Anyway, he's retired now."

There was a long pause. Purbright looked thoughtful.

"Who took that inquest? The regular coroner, wasn't it?"

"Mr. Cannon. Yes, it was."

"Open verdict?"

"Yes."

"The Croll family . . . weren't they represented by Mr. Loughbury?"

"I think they were. Yes, I remember him sitting in court with Ben Croll. And when you say family, that's it—just Ben; there aren't any others."

"Your friend the bar lady—Miss Howell: she wasn't called as a witness, was she?"

Love said no.

"Then I wonder why she should think of her child in connexion with Mrs. Croll. I don't remember anything about a boy giving evidence."

"There wasn't a kid at the inquest. Mr. Larch did some interviewing beforehand, though." Love added: "He was an expert at not believing."

"Perhaps Bill will know. I'll have a word with him later."

Love waited, retriever-like. Not for the first time, the inspector was visited with the ridiculous temptation to pat his head.

Mrs. Zoe Claypole-Loughbury had been spending the morning much more constructively than might have been expected of so recent a widow.

At ten o'clock she telephoned, and was shortly afterwards attended by, Mr. Clapper Buxton, confidential clerk of Loughbury, Lovelace and Partners. In the interval before his arrival, she made two further telephone calls. The first was to Mr. Harrington, manager of Gallery Ganby, to whom she wished to entrust the compilation of an inventory and valuation. Mr. Harrington said he would be delighted to comply with her wishes; might he call that evening and discuss preliminary arrangements? Zoe said sure, he could please himself, so long as he made a proper job of it and didn't muck about too long. Then she rang the Flaxborough *Citizen* to say she wanted to insert a thanks notice worth quite a few quid and would they send somebody over pronto so that the words were got right.

Mr. George Robert Buxton, encouraged by the hour to dream of biscuits and coffee and ladies in negligées, came straight in on finding the front door unlatched.

Clapper would not have been everyone's idea of a lawyer's clerk. Rather on the bouncy side, and self-indulgent in respect of dress, which usually included a bow tie and fancy socks, he dealt with the clients in so confident a manner, and with so little sign of deference, that many at first supposed him to be the mysterious Lovelace or, at any rate, one of the Partners. He never corrected these little misunderstandings; indeed, as time went on, he himself came to be persuaded that the corporate wisdom and authority of the firm, after gradual transmigration from persons of greater title but lesser worth, now resided fully within his own breast.

"Are you there, dear lady?" inquired Mr. Buxton loudly from just inside the front door.

Receiving no reply, he proceeded at once from room to room on the ground floor until he discovered Zoe in the kitchen. She was eating the first of three slices of fried bread and reading a newspaper.

"Ah, so this is where we are, dear lady."

Zoe put down the paper, but not the bread, and elbowed some sundries to the back of the table. "Cup of tea?"

Clapper glanced at where the negligée should have been and saw a kind of goalkeeper's jersey. Of biscuits the table was innocent. "Tea?" he repeated, dubiously. She did not respond, *Or coffee.* He raised his hand in token of high-minded abstinence, then busied himself with the catch of his briefcase.

"Sit down," invited Zoe through a mouthful of fried bread. "Here—shove your stuff on the table."

From outside came the buzz and clatter of a motor. Mrs. Claypole could be seen through the window, mowing the lawn. At the turns, she had to circle at a run to keep up with the machine. She looked hot and somewhat distressed.

Zoe watched Mr. Buxton withdraw a sheaf of papers from his case and lay it carefully before him. "That's the old spondooliks, is it?"

"I think," he said, "you can take it that we have here the final testamentary disposition of your, of the late, Mr. Loughbury."

"His will, you mean?"

Clapper sucked in a little air. "Will? Yes—oh, yes, will. You could call it that."

Zoe reached over and tugged free one of the pages. She felt the stiff thickness of the parchment and squinted at its elaborate engrossment.

"Good grief," she said softly.

Clapper looked pleased. "It will be subject to probate, of course, but I do not anticipate any great difficulty."

"I should think not," said Zoe. "It would be a poor do if a solicitor couldn't make his own will."

From Clapper came "Ha ha." It sounded as if he were reading it.

"As the late Mr. Loughbury will perhaps have told you," Mr. Buxton said, "you are virtually the sole beneficiary. Certain bequests have been made in other directions, naturally, but they amount to very little proportionately."

"You mean I more or less cop the lot," Zoe deciphered.

Clapper said nothing, but scratched his nose and

looked again at Zoe's unpromising woollen garment. From a point level with his nose, a finger descended, slowly tracing one of the deep runnels in the clerk's long, gaunt face. He was debating whether he ought to chance his arm with a risqué remark.

Zoe took his silence to mean yes. She nodded, ran her tongue between teeth and cheeks in pursuit of fried bread fragments, and picked up a second slice. "Well, that's all right, then. Oh, by the way . . ."

"Mmmm?" purred Mr. Buxton, with a smile that hinted at a dissolute other self. He had never interviewed a lady client at breakfast before.

"I've fixed up with this bloke to do a proper pricing job on Dick's bits and pieces." She saw his smile fade. "His collection. The pictures and that."

After the smile, a frown. "Bloke?" Clapper repeated, not at all seductively. "What bloke?"

She told him, while she poured herself another cup of tea.

"I'm not at all sure," said Mr. Buxton, "that the Partners would have advised you to do that." His sudden adoption of a disapproving attitude had the curious effect of stiffening even more the crop of thick greyish-yellow hair that grew, brushlike, atop the long, flat-ended head.

"That's all right. They're not going to be asked."

"I'm not sure that Mr. Richard would have cared for the idea either. Some of his collection involved transactions of a fairly delicate nature." A moment went by. "Or so I understand," Clapper added carefully.

Zoe looked round the table for tomato sauce. She spread some on the last slice of bread.

"You mean he got them by a fiddle?" she inquired equably.

"I mean nothing of the kind." Clapper was sitting so erect that his chair creaked. "The point I wished to make is that the Partners have their own arrangements in respect of valuation business."

Zoe licked some sauce from her forefinger, which she then poked into Mr. Buxton's chest. "*You* thought you'd get a backhander from the assessors, right?"

He stood. He was very angry. He grasped the briefcase, open, in his left hand, his intention to sweep the documents into it with his right. He had not noticed that the teapot had been set down by Zoe on top of the will. He now waited magisterially for her to remove it. She didn't.

After a while, she said: "Not that I was thinking of selling any of the boodle. You need it in a house like this one." She looked about her. "There'll be a lot more entertaining to do from now on."

Tight-lipped, Clapper moved the teapot himself. He picked up the documents and was about to put them in his case.

"Right," said Zoe, wiping her mouth with one hand and suddenly tugging the will away from him with the other, "let's see what the fairies have left, shall we?"

CHAPTER 8

Sergeant William Malley, the coroner's officer, kept his inquests upon three shelves on the dry south wall of the room he occupied in the basement of Flaxborough police headquarters. They were in excellent condition, even the earliest of them, dating back to just after the war, when the coroner had been old Amblesby with his clicky teeth and his free weighs on the morgue scales.

The written records—the depositions, medical reports, coroner's notes—were kept in strong, flat cardboard boxes. In these, too, were interred photographs and the more manageable exhibits, together with references to the whereabouts of items too cumbersome or too unsavoury to remain in a small office.

"Small" had special meaning in the context of Sergeant Malley, who would have looked cramped in a bullring. He did not so much occupy his office as wear it. It was like an outer uniform, rather tight round the shoulders and with nothing to spare at the waist, but long and familiar use had enabled him to adjust so happily to its limitations that he now could even entertain a fellow occupant without undue distress.

"Croll, Croll, Croll . . ." Half-turned in his chair and breathing hard, Malley reviewed his collection on the third shelf. "Ah . . ." He hooked a finger round the back of a box and reached it down.

Purbright, seated at the opposite side of Malley's desk, watched him slide off a pair of elastic bands and unlid the box. He put the bands in the lid and placed both in a filing tray. For so large a man, the sergeant had small, neat, capable hands; they always moved slowly and to the purpose.

Malley produced a photograph from the box. He did not, as many a colleague might have done, flip it to Purbright like a playing card, but set it gently before him. Malley's knowledge of those with whose end he had had to deal was wide, sometimes comical, often squalid, but his manner towards them was unfailingly respectful.

The inspector gazed at the picture of Bernadette Croll (1939–1980), housewife, of Home Farm, Mumblesby. It was a police photograph in black and white, taken in the mortuary of Flaxborough General Hospital before the autopsy. Meticulously in focus, the body was lighted as if shadow was against the law. The torso and limbs had the curious appearance of having been modelled not in flesh but in rather dirty lard. Even the smallest blemish, the least significant bruise, looked black and sinister.

"No children, were there?" Purbright asked. He did not look up.

Malley said, "No, no kids."

She was not a fat woman, not plump even. There was a suggestion of flaccidity about the thighs and belly, but the small breasts and narrow shoulders could have been those of someone much younger.

"Benjamin Croll—what do you know about him, Bill?"

"Not a lot. Farmer. Rich. Middling miserable. In his sixties now." Malley gave a small snort of amusement. "I doubt if he's still up to chucking blokes out of the bedroom window."

Purbright remembered, grinned. "Christ, aye! Of course, that was Ben, wasn't it. And the phoney M15 man."

"Long time ago." Malley made it sound like a gentle reproof. He began filling his pipe.

The face in the photograph was like that of an old child. The expression might have been described as one of utter indifference, save that the angle of the head (it was slightly, but disconcertingly, awry) was somehow suggestive of the anxiety and effort of someone hard of hearing.

"It's easy to see her neck was broken," Malley said. He pointed with his pipestem.

Purbright saw also the patch of almost black bruising over the upper area of the side of the woman's face, from brow to cheekbone. The eye was within it, dead yet returning the camera flash. The half-open lids had a beaten sulkiness about them.

There were other photographs, taken inside the church. One showed the area beneath the tower where Bernadette Croll's body had been found. A chalk outline had been drawn on the floor.

Malley noticed the inspector looking at the outline. "That's more or less a guess," he said. "The body had been moved by the time Harton got out there."

Purbright looked at two more pictures. One, taken from the ground, was of the tower interior. A cross had been marked against a narrow balustraded gallery about two thirds of the way up to the floor of the ringing chamber. The second picture was simply the reverse view: the floor of the tower, seen from the gallery.

"Do X-rays mean anything to you?" Malley asked.

"I'm no radiologist."

The sergeant held to the light a rectangle of black film. Silvery lines and patches appeared, the pale map of a skull. Purbright wondered at the smallness, the insubstantiality of the image.

Malley pointed to something. Purbright thought he

could detect the faintest of irregularities, but wasn't
sure.

"According to Heinemann," Malley said, "that's a
fracture." He pointed lower down. "And that's the
neck dislocation."

"Which one killed her?"

"The skull fracture, Heinemann said. There was a lot
of brain haemorrhaging. Anyway, here's the postmortem report, if you want to read it." He drew out of
the box a closely typed foolscap sheet.

Purbright glanced at it, put it aside. "Let's look at
some of the statements. I wasn't here at the time."

Malley sorted out another sheet of typescript and
handed it across the desk. "Best start at the beginning," he said. "Discovery of body. And who better to
make it than a man with a name like that?"

Robin Hugh Lestrange Bradden Cork-Bradden had
testified:

I reside at Church House, Mumblesby. I am a
retired army officer and I hold a number of company directorships. For the past eight years I have
been Vicar's Warden at the parish church of St.
Dennis the Martyr. In that capacity, I have the
custody of one of the two church keys and it is my
responsibility to lock the church at the end of the
day and to open it again each morning.

At about nine-thirty in the evening of Thursday,
August the twenty-first, 1980, I locked the south
door after making sure the church was empty.
This is my customary precaution. All the doors
other than the south door are kept locked perma-
nently. I had no need that evening to switch on
the church lights, as there was still adequate daylight.

Shortly before ten o'clock the next morning, Friday, I went again to the church, this time in com-

pany with Mr. Raymond Bishop, whom I had happened to meet on my way. I unlocked the south door and looked inside. I was surprised to see what I took to be a bundle of cassocks lying on the floor. On closer examination, I found it to be the body of Mrs. Croll. Mr. Bishop went for help. I could see Mrs. Croll was dead. [In reply to the coroner] I had no doubts at all. As a soldier, I know death when I see it.

Questioned by Superintendent Larch, Mr. Cork-Bradden said the body was lying near an old iron-bound box known as the church chest. He agreed that the position of the body was consistent with Mrs. Croll's having fallen from the gallery in the tower, access to which was by a staircase in the tower wall. The door to the staircase was never locked. Witness agreed that his evening search of the church, though not perfunctory, would be unlikely to disclose anyone deliberately hiding.

In answer to Mr. Richard Loughbury, representing the Croll family, witness said he had conversed on a few occasions with deceased. She had seemed to hold deeply religious views. The subject obsessed her. The conversations, some of which had been at witness's home, had not been of his seeking. They had not embarrassed him; he had felt sorry for her and had tried to be helpful.

"It seems to me," said Purbright to Malley, "that Mr. Croll's legal representative was less coy on the subject of Mrs. Croll's mental state than one might have expected. You notice that Loughbury quite openly led Cork-Bradden into suggesting the woman was missing a few marbles."

"Perhaps she was."

"Perhaps—but relatives never admit these things.

They're felt to reflect discredit on the family. Let's have a look at the husband's evidence, anyway."

Benjamin Croll, farmer, of Home Farm, Mumblesby, said that he had been shown a body in the mortuary of Flaxborough General Hospital and recognised it as that of his wife, Bernadette Croll. He had last seen his wife alive at half-past eleven, on the previous Friday morning—dinnertime. She had eaten her meal and left the house, saying she would be back to get him his tea, but she had not returned by bedtime, and he heard no more until the police telephoned him the following morning.

In reply to the coroner, witness said he had not been worried; his wife had stayed out all night on previous occasions. Answering Mr. Loughbury, witness further stated that his wife had lately become very religious and had told him that she stayed out at night to keep God company He agreed that it would be consistent with his wife's attitude of mind if she had concealed herself in the parish church in order to pray on her own until morning.

Witness Croll, questioned by Superintendent Larch, said his wife had twice before threatened to take her own life, but because she was so religious he did not think she meant it.

"There you are, then," said Malley. "Ben certainly thought his missus was round the twist. He could scarcely have put it more plainly."

"Did you ever have anything to do with her, Bill?"

"Took a statement from her once. Must be nearly twenty years ago, though."

Purbright smiled. "You are going to say you remember nothing about her."

Malley wheezed protestingly. "If I'm supposed to remember everybody who ever came into this office . . ."

"Bill, a long time ago it may be, but don't tell me you've forgotten somebody of whom you said at the time—and I quote—'That girl's had more ferret than I've had hot dinners.'"

"Aye, well . . ." The sergeant looked down and rubbed the bowl of his pipe with his thumb. "Perhaps we take too much notice of what people say."

"Wasn't it true, then?"

"You know what villages are."

"I'm not sure that I do. Not Mumblesby, anyway. Now come on, was the woman promiscuous or was she not?"

"She isn't now, that's for certain." Malley saw the beginning of a frown of exasperation. He said quickly and with a note of grumpiness: "Of course she was. She was on the batter. You know bloody well!"

Purbright disliked harrying the sergeant, whose occasional obstructiveness came of a purely quixotic desire to protect those who could not help themselves. He wanted to explain the reason for his line of questioning, but he was not yet sure himself what it was.

He asked: "When was she supposed to have taken to religion?"

Malley stared gloomily at the mortuary photograph and shook his head. "No idea. First I heard of that was at the inquest." He looked up at Purbright. "She left Ben a couple of times—you know that?"

"I did not."

"Aye. Once with a car salesman from Grantham. The other was that art teacher at Flaxborough evening classes. They reckoned there were others, but I wouldn't know."

"How recent was the last affair that you *did* know about?"

Malley considered. "That would be the art bloke

. . . oh, about six months before she was killed. A year maybe."

The inspector was silent for some moments.

"Something you said just now, Bill . . ."

"Aye?"

"You said the first you heard about Bernadette's religious conversion, or mania, or whatever it was, was during the inquest. Did you mean that literally? Actually *during* the inquest?"

"Yes, why?"

The inspector looked at some pages of the record. "It seems to have come out in response to questions—mainly questions put by Loughbury to the husband and to Cork-Bradden."

"That's right."

"So it wasn't mentioned by any of these people at any time while you were taking their depositions *before* the inquest?"

"Not a dickeybird."

"Odd," said Purbright.

"In what way?"

"Simply that here is a woman, considered by two people at least, one of them her own husband, to be a religious nut, who is found dead in a church, of all places. That isn't the sort of coincidence that requires a lawyer to spot. Why didn't somebody say straight out: Oh, yes, just the sort of thing she *would* do?"

"I suppose they were all taking the charitable view."

Purbright stared. "Oh, Bill, come on . . ."

He said no more until he had read the testimony of the final witness, a young constable who contrived to include so many measurements in his report that the actual distance of the woman's fall was crowded out and needed to be established by further calculation. Purbright made it forty-two feet.

The constable also had searched the gallery and

there discovered a handbag, subsequently identified as the property of deceased. The bag had contained, according to Superintendent Larch's remark to the coroner, who had recorded it, "nothing suggestive of why Mrs. Croll was in the church or how she came to fall from the gallery."

Purbright looked up. "Right about that, was he, Bill —the handbag contents?"

Reluctantly, Malley confirmed the correctness of interloper Larch's judgement. The bag had held a purse and money, a chequebook, cosmetics, handkerchief, car keys, cigarettes and lighter.

A receipt for these things and for the clothing his wife had been wearing at the time bore the signature of Benjamin Croll. Also listed were two rings, a silver chain necklace and one earring.

"*One* earring?"

"Yes," said Malley. "The other has never been found. It presumably had rolled into a crevice or down one of the gratings."

The sergeant packed into the box all the documents but the medical report. Purbright motioned him to take that also: he seemed to have lost much of his interest. Malley packed everything in and secured the lid with the two rubber bands.

Suddenly Purbright said: "I want to know about a young boy named Howell. His mother's a barmaid at the Mumblesby pub."

Malley took his time putting the box back in its place on the shelf. He was smiling, as at the memory of some once familiar but harmless nuisance.

"What have they been telling you about young Oggy Howell, then?"

"His mother seems to think there's a connection between Mrs. Croll's death and what she sees as a threat to take the boy away from her."

Malley stroked one of his chins. "You realise the kid's not very bright?"

"I know nothing about him."

"I don't mean he's batty. Nothing like that. But I think he spends a lot of the time in a little world of his own. His mother brought him in here and I tried talking to him, but he could never have been put up as a witness. Larch more or less booted them both out."

"Why?"

The sergeant puffed his cheeks. "Well, you know Larch. He's not very tolerant of what we call one-parent families nowadays. They're all fallen women to the superintendent."

"So you've no record of what was said."

Malley shook his head.

"Did any of it make sense?"

"Not a lot. I don't doubt the kid was there and peeking into the church through one of the windows."

"At what time would that be?"

"Between eleven and midnight, his mother said. It was just before twelve o'clock that he came in. She was having supper. He had some with her and tried to tell her about something he'd seen."

"How old is Oggy?"

Malley pouted. "About ten."

"A late little bird."

The sergeant said he did not doubt it.

"All right. Now tell me what Oggy said he saw."

"You really want me to?"

Purbright waited. Malley was busy once more with his pipe ritual. It was not often, the inspector realised, that he had seen him actually smoking it.

"For what it's worth," Malley said at last, "the kid's story was that there was a lady in the church who was going to do the washing . . ."

"She was what?"

Malley sighed. "I warned you."

"Sorry. Go on. The lady was about to do the washing."

"Right. And she was reading off a card how to do it. But then a big bird came and blew the candle out."

"Blew the candle out," Purbright repeated woodenly.

"Yes."

"A big bird."

"That's right."

There was a long silence. Purbright sighed.

"I have no intention," he said, "of reopening one of Mr. Larch's inquests. I certainly don't want to cross-examine imaginative little boys who don't get enough sleep. But I should love to know what that one really saw."

"I don't think there's much mystery about the bird," Malley said. "It can only have been poor Bernadette."

"On her way down?"

"Aye. He'll have been so scared that he'd need to make up an explanation that he could cope with."

"And the washing?" Purbright challenged. "The card the lady was reading?"

"Oggy's mother tried to be helpful there," said the sergeant. "She said she keeps a card of instructions pinned to a shelf above the washing machine at home so the kid associates reading with washing."

"And where does that lead us?"

Malley shrugged.

"Did Miss Howell offer any suggestions?" the inspector asked.

For the first time in the conversation, Malley looked less than perfectly calm.

"Mothers," he said, "always come up with something to justify their children. Sadie Howell tried to get Larch to believe that if Oggy said he'd seen a lady reading by candlelight, then that's exactly what he *had* seen, and that if it was Mrs. Croll in the church, then it must have been Mrs. Croll that he'd watched reading."

Purbright considered briefly, then shook his head.

"I don't see why we should quarrel with that. What the woman was doing before she climbed to the gallery and fell isn't necessarily significant."

"That's all very well," said Malley, "but Sadie tried to sell us the big bird story as well. She got it into her head that Mrs. Croll hadn't gone up the tower at all but had been attacked there where she was standing."

"Attacked?"

"By somebody who rushed at her. Swooped like a bird, in fact."

The inspector stared. "What on earth gave her that idea?"

Malley struck a match and regarded the flame thoughtfully. "There's something we have to remember. Miss Howell had more than ordinary cause to stand by Oggy's story once he'd started going round telling it to people."

The match had nearly burned out; he dropped it into a little jar on his desk and struck another. "She was scared that if ever there was a question about him not being all there, he might be taken away from her."

"But there'd have to be an application on behalf of the local authority to get him into care."

With great concentration, Malley sucked fire into the pipe bowl, then barbecued the end of his forefinger. "After the inquest, Sadie wrote a letter to the chief constable apologising for wasting police time. She said the boy had made it all up and was sorry."

"That could have been the truth of the matter, Bill."

"Superintendent Larch thought so."

"And you didn't?" Purbright was watching Malley's face.

"Me? I'm just the coroner's tea boy. I don't tell the C.I.O. what to do."

"I should think not," Purbright agreed amiably. He stretched, looked at his watch.

There had to be endured a little more pipe play on the part of the Wise Old Peasant, then Malley (he had a tucked-in, adenoidal way of speaking on these occasions) sniffed, regarded his hands and remarked to the ball of his left thumb: "Of course, it suited Mr. Larch not to listen to Oggy's tale."

"Oh?"

The right thumb was addressed. "Midnight, locked church, lights off at the main switch—as they were still in the morning." Malley looked up. "Well, there was nothing to explain. Everything straightforward."

"Much more satisfactory, I should have thought," said Purbright, "than having to explain midnight laundry and big birds and candles."

"And candle grease," added Malley, with such studied concern that he dropped his pipe.

CHAPTER 9

Purbright had not expected much success in the matter of the candlewax traces. A parish church, even in an era of declining religious observance, is trodden by many visitors in a year. But there they were—dark discs on the stone. They had survived the passage of feet by virtue of having fallen in the shelter of the font plinth.

The inspector, squatting to take a close look at them, heard the raising of the latch, then the cushioned close of the south door. He did not get up. Footsteps approached, firm, businesslike, proprietorial.

"Good afternoon." The Reverend Alan Kiverton gazed upon the half-kneeling Purbright with a mixture of inquiry and high benevolence. "There is no objection to you people taking rubbings, you know. We do rather prefer you to ask permission, of course, but, as I say, there's no objection. Carry on."

The inspector got up. "In point of fact . . ." he began.

At once, Mr. Kiverton's smile contracted to an O of recognition and he held forth his hand like a wrestler.

"My dear Mr. Purfleet, forgive me. I did not recognise our knight-errant of the other day."

Purbright took both the compliment and the misnomer in good part and inquired after the rescued lady's health.

"In the pink," declared the vicar. "Or so I understand."

"An unfortunate time for such a misadventure," the inspector suggested.

"Indeed, yes. Mmm. Rather." Mr. Kiverton had an interesting talent for sounding keen to prolong a conversation while in the very act of abandoning it. Already he was moving away from the inspector.

"Brass rubbings . . ." Purbright produced the words quickly, as a sort of holding device.

"Mmm?" The vicar halted and turned upon him an eyes-closed smile of solicitude.

". . . are not at all my line, I'm afraid."

The vicar's eyes opened. He glanced down to where the inspector had been kneeling.

"Oh, dear. Not detection, I trust?" Behind the mildly fatuous good humour was something of anxiety.

"Hardly that, Mr. Kiverton. I was simply wondering how candle grease had come to be dropped so far from the altar. A Corpus Christi procession perhaps?"

"God forbid," exclaimed Mr. Kiverton piously. He peered at the spot. "Do you know, I'd never noticed it before. No, no, a procession couldn't have been responsible. There'd have been a trail, not a group. You see? All together. These are drips from a candle held still and over a period."

He straightened, boyishly pleased with himself. "There, now—what do you want solving next?"

Purbright smiled at the pleasantry, then immediately looked aloft.

"Hell of a way to commit suicide."

Mr. Kiverton looked startled, then grave.

"Any method of suicide is the hell of a way." He said it slowly and with careful enunciation. Purbright gave the line full marks.

"She was a parishioner of yours, was she, Mrs. Croll?"

"A parishioner, yes; a communicant, no." The vicar

waited a moment. "Of course, I cannot speak of the years before my arrival here." A further pause. "Incidentally, the verdict at the inquest was an open one. I do not feel it would be right to ascribe suicidal intention to the poor woman, whatever her past transgressions."

"Her reputation," said Purbright, "was that of a very devout person."

Mr. Kiverton clasped his hands and nodded. "That is most gratifying," he said. "It costs us nothing to think well of the dead."

Suddenly he was in striding motion along the nave. As he drew away, he raised his hand in farewell.

Purbright waited for the vicar to pass through a curtained door at the east end, then unhurriedly looked about him.

The fifteenth-century chest, with its three locks and its strappings and corners of iron, occupied a position between the tower and the big ornamental font. It was a formidable piece of furniture, built to thwart robbers and time. Purbright stroked the black, ice-cold edge of its iron. Deadly enough, certainly, to wreak execution at the end of a fall.

He looked up at the distant gallery, pictured the woman's descent, a parabola, the body upright at first but turning in the plunge. Her head must have been struck by that edge with force enough to cleave it. Must? Well, no, not necessarily. Or there would have been more mess. Bone thickness was an unpredictable factor.

He remembered the boy. The retraction of his story, queer though it was, did not ring true. Oggy, weak-witted or no, had almost certainly been watching when the woman jumped. Through which window, though, had he peeped?

There were four possibilities, all lancet windows,

plainly glazed; two in the south wall, two in the north, directly opposite.

Purbright left the church and began to walk round it, keeping close to the wall. Beneath the lancet windows on the south side was a monumental family tomb, about three feet high. An energetic ten-year-old would have no difficulty in scrambling to its flat top.

Standing with the tomb at his back, the inspector looked through the left-hand window. Even in the relative darkness of the church, he could easily discern the chest, the font, with its massive, elaborately carved cover, and the nearest two pillars of the nave.

He walked round the west end of the church to where the wall was pierced by the opposite, matching pair of lancet windows.

The ground was lower here, the windows harder to reach. The Howell boy would not have found this place much use as a vantage point. In any case, he would have needed to risk observation from the back windows of a house only a few yards away.

Purbright stepped back to take a fuller view of the window. Something crunched beneath his heel. He glanced down and saw the glitter of glass; a few fragments lay widespread about the narrow path. Again he looked up at the window.

At its very apex, scarcely noticeable from ground level, one of the little panes was missing.

Purbright returned to the south porch and reentered the church. The vicar was leaning over a baize-topped table near the door, arranging pamphlets and postcards. There was a box on the table, slotted for coins. Purbright dropped in a fifty-pence piece and took possession of "The Story of St. Dennis and His Church" by the Reverend E. Cherry-Morgan.

Mr. Kiverton beamed approval. "One of my predecessors," he explained. "Not that he'll get fat on the royalties, I fear." And he replaced the inspector's copy with one he took from a cardboard box that once had held a dozen of Pale Fino sherry.

"Did you know you have a broken window?" Purbright asked.

The vicar's face clouded at once. "Oh, dear—at the vicarage, you mean?"

"No, here."

Mr. Kiverton looked relieved. He followed Purbright's glance to the top of the lancet.

"That," the vicar said, "was done quite a while ago— oh, last year sometime. The diocesan architect . . ." He paused, vaguely sensible of the inspector's having inserted a small question somewhere. "I beg your pardon?"

"I said, How? How did it come to be broken?"

"Boys, I suppose." Mr. Kiverton, who had fathered four daughters, brushed back a lock of his light-brown, healthy-looking hair. "Boys are always throwing things."

"But not inside churches, surely?"

"One would hope not."

"That window," said Purbright, "was not broken by a stone thrown from outside. The pieces of glass are still out there on the path."

"Really? Do you know, I'd never given the matter much thought. That is rather odd, though, now that you mention it."

"If he was actually trying for the top pane, he must have been a singularly good shot," the inspector remarked.

"Shot?" A note almost of alarm had entered the vicar's voice.

"I mean with a stone. An accurate throw, in other words."

"Ah. I had begun to visualise rifle practice or something of that sort."

For several seconds, Purbright said no more. He continued to stare upward, but now with a frown of concentration. The vicar, who noted the frown, remained silent also.

"Do you happen to have a ladder handy, Mr. Kiverton?"

The vicar, now pleasurably curious, fetched an eight-foot aluminium ladder from a storage recess in the base of the tower. Purbright set the ladder against the wall close by the lancet window, shifted it to and fro once or twice, shook it dubiously and, with the vicar pledged to hold it steady, climbed with extreme caution as far as the fifth rung.

When he descended, he insisted on helping the vicar to carry the ladder back to its store.

There were other things in the recess, which was concealed behind a long, wine-coloured curtain. Purbright saw an ancient vacuum cleaner, four tarnished vases, some brooms and a bucket, and several structures in lightweight wrought iron, painted black.

One of these engaged his particular attention. It supported at head height a small wooden notice board, in which a few rusty drawing pins survived. The simple sconce attached to the edge of the board still held in its socket a remnant of candle, two or three inches long and ribbed with the wax that had run from it.

Purbright said nothing about these things. He spoke instead of his examination of the window.

"I just wanted to be quite sure," he said, "that there was no question of a firearm having been used. One doesn't like to think there might be someone around who'd take pot shots in a church."

"Ah, the celebrated forensic tests. And up a ladder too. This is quite my day."

Purbright smiled modestly.

"You can tell, can you," asked blithe Mr. Kiverton, "whether it was a bullet that passed through, or just a stone? How extraordinary."

The inspector shrugged and said something that sounded like "peripheral vitreous deposits." Then he changed the subject.

"Tell me, Vicar, who lives in that rather attractive old house over the way?"

"Church House, you mean? Tudor, mostly. As you say, rather attractive. Would that it were still the vicarage, alas. Who lives there, did you say? The Cork-Braddens."

"Handy for him."

"Handy?"

"He's your churchwarden, isn't he? Mr. Cork-Bradden."

"Ah, I see what you mean. Handy. Yes, of course."

Mr. Kiverton was beginning to display once more that anxiety to be about his Father's business which Purbright found strongly suggestive of a car at traffic lights—an impression enhanced by his frequent "hmm-hmm's," as if some impatient foot were tapping his accelerator.

Before giving him green, so to speak, the inspector introduced one final subject of inquiry. Was the vicar acquainted, by any chance, with a curiosity that had come into the collection of the late Mr. Loughbury—a piece of timber that purported to be a sacred relic of some kind?

There was no mistaking Mr. Kiverton's healthily Anglican disdain of Romish superstition. He threw back his head and laughed aloud.

"Oh, dear, that ridiculous bit of wood! You saw it, did you? In that sort of cage thing? Gracious, yes, hmm. Oh, I'm afraid he had his odd side, did our neighbour Loughbury. Or a bizarre sense of humour. Hmm."

"But not every collector's item, surely, is necessarily genuine in an intrinsic sense. Even a bogus article can be valuable if its associations are sufficiently interesting."

Mr. Kiverton smiled into the middle distance. "I still incline to the hope that the late Mr. Loughbury was having a joke." The smile faded. "I would rather think that, than impugn the man's honesty."

"Is that the alternative?"

The vicar regarded Purbright thoughtfully for a moment. "I take it that you don't know much about the history of this thing?"

The inspector said he knew nothing.

"Very well, let me 'fill you in,' as they say. You are aware, are you not, that Loughbury was a fairly diligent collector of objets d'art—within his means, of course."

Purbright said he had seen and admired a number of articles at the Manor House.

Kiverton nodded. "And very nice they are. But now let me tell you about the 'lump of firewood,' as my wife rather unkindly described Loughbury's celebrated relic.

"It turned up last year—oh, about the end of the summer, I think it was. Where he got it from, I've no idea. Nor do I know what he was persuaded to pay for it. His own estimate of its value was so ridiculous that I cannot now call it to mind. Some thousands of pounds anyway. A London firm of so-called security experts caged it for him. And there it was, on the wall in that upstairs room, as if it was Magna Carta or something." The vicar, who was leaning against the font, shifted his elbow to a more comfortable position amidst the carvings on the cover.

"It is what Loughbury did next that rather disturbs me. He invited a number of people in Mumblesby—not many, but several of the more well-to-do, I should say—to a private view of this marvel of his. Moreover—and this is the whole point—these people were asked to make donations towards what he called 'keeping a priceless relic within our village.'"

"To give him money, you mean?"

"Oh, no. The letter of invitation—it was a duplicated thing, but nicely done, I remember—suggested that what it called tax complications could be avoided by making contributions 'in kind.'"

Purbright raised his brows. "Did you not think this a somewhat questionable approach, Mr. Kiverton?"

The vicar looked pained. "Well, I do *now*, naturally, but I don't think I took an awful lot of notice at the time. We were very busy with one thing and another, and of course there'd been that dreadful accident, and then the inquest, and so on."

"I take it that you, yourself, were not asked by Mr. Loughbury to make a contribution?"

"I? Oh, dear, no." The vicar grinned roguishly. "That would have been rather like offering someone shares in his own company."

"Unauthenticated shares, at that."

"Ha! Ha! Yes, indeed. Very good."

The inspector asked no more questions. He parted from Mr. Kiverton in an atmosphere of almost jovial goodwill. To what extent this cordiality had been generated by his own reticence he was unable to judge. He could not help wondering, though, as he left the church, if the vicar would be quite so cheerful had he been told what closer examination of the broken window had revealed.

CHAPTER 10

The chief constable, unlike the vicar, could not be left in ignorance, euphoric or otherwise. The very next morning, Purbright sought out Mr. Chubb in his room at the Fen Street headquarters.

As it was Friday, the chief constable was engaged in the self-appointed task, peculiar to that day of the week, of reading the Flaxborough *Citizen*. This he did most methodically, standing before the table on which the newspaper was spread, and perusing it line by line, column after column, page by page, with the aid of a large, square reading glass. He looked rather like a bomb-disposal expert with lots of time.

"Sit down, Mr. Purbright."

The inspector did so, but at a sufficient distance to minimise the chief constable's moral advantage of remaining standing.

"I am just casting an eye over poor Loughbury's funeral," said Mr. Chubb. He put aside his ocular mine-detector and frowned. "I see that you attended as the representative of a Mr. Crumb."

Purbright, whom custom had led to accept as unremarkable the fitfulness of the *Citizen*'s presentation of names and places, offered no remark. The chief constable put down his lens as a marker of the place he had reached and crossed to the fireplace, against which he leaned in a posture of austere but courteous attention.

"I fear," Purbright began, "that my doubts of all

being as it should be at Mumblesby are beginning to
be justified."

"Mumblesby?" Mr. Chubb's brows rose. "Whatever
has been going on at Mumblesby?"

Without abandoning any of his customary solemnity,
Mr. Chubb made the most of the name's comic over-
tones. He was capable of conferring an almost fictional
quality upon any place or person he did not wish to
talk about.

Purbright nodded, as if with deep satisfaction.

"I felt sure you would be anxious to know that, sir.
The answer cannot be as full at this stage as you would
wish, unfortunately, but several significant facts have
come to light, and I think they ought to be made
known to you straightaway."

"Of course, Mr. Purbright. Please go on."

The inspector did so. First, he recapitulated his own
misgivings concerning the fire at the Manor House.
Then he gave an edited version of Love's gleanings
from village conversation. The more pertinent of Malley's addenda to the Croll inquest record were quoted.
Finally, Mr. Chubb heard what the Vicar of Mumblesby had not yet been told about the hole in his
church window.

It was the last item which seemed to put the severest
strain on the chief constable's comprehension.

"I'm sorry, but I do not quite see the significance of
this glass business. You say the pane had been *cut*
out. Not broken—*cut*."

"Yes, sir. When you get close enough, you can see
the clean edge of the glass left behind in the lead setting. It forms a sort of border. There's a scratch in one
place where the cutter must have slipped, but no
cracks, no sign of shattering."

"And you think that whoever did this was inside the
church?"

"The fragments of broken glass were on the ground outside. That does suggest that the cut-away portion was pushed outward, not inward. In any case, the scratch I mentioned was on the inner surface."

The chief constable was already resigned to the unlikelihood of his being able to deflect Purbright from his collision course towards the sleeping dogs of Mumblesby. He was still unsure, however, as to what crime or crimes the inspector intended to postulate.

"Odd business," said Mr. Chubb, looking for dust on his jacket sleeve.

"Odd, sir?"

"This cutting holes in church windows. It doesn't seem to have any logical connection with anything."

"Not immediately, perhaps, sir. But any act which is difficult in itself and which entails trouble and some degree of risk can fairly safely be assumed to have been undertaken for a purpose."

The chief constable acknowledged the lecture with a wintry smile. "You know, Mr. Purbright, I have the feeling that your researches at Mumblesby are not going to content you until you find a rifle with telescopic sights to go with that peephole of yours."

Purbright affected serious consideration.

"No, sir. Your theory has certain attractions, but I don't think the pathologist could have misinterpreted a bullet wound. In any case, if Mrs. Croll stood where I believe she did, practically the whole mass of the font and its cover would have stood between her and the prepared hole in the lancet window."

Mr. Chubb essayed nothing further in the irony line.

"Perhaps it would be as well," he said, "if you were to set out—in a general sort of way—your reasons for wanting to reopen this affair. One has to be terribly careful in matters that have been officially cleared up, you understand. Coroners don't like inquests to be called into question, and they can be very awkward."

Purbright said he did understand. The fact remained that the circumstances of Mrs. Croll's death were far more suspicious than witnesses at the inquest had suggested. If, as he now had reason to suspect, the woman had neither committed suicide nor died accidentally, it was urgent—if only for the protection of others—that the true facts be established.

"I take it that you believe the woman was attacked," said the chief constable.

"I am convinced that she was."

"But for what reason, Mr. Purbright? A perfectly harmless married woman—a farmer's wife—with strong religious convictions . . . Why should anyone wish to kill Mrs. Croll?"

"Why should she have wished to kill herself, sir?"

Mr. Chubb waved his hand vaguely. "Who can say? Nervous trouble? Change of life?"

The menopause loomed as large in the chief constable's catalogue of mischief-makers as central heating and socialism.

"She was forty-one," the inspector said simply. He added: "So far as records in such things can be established, she had not entered a church—for other than libidinous purposes—since the age of thirteen."

Mr. Chubb frowned. He looked annoyed.

"I suppose I have to take your word for all this, Mr. Purbright. Even so, we are a long way from being able to assume that an attack was made on the woman. She was alone in the place, according to the only evidence I can recall."

"Yes, sir, but it was conceded that she could have been hiding when the church was locked for the night. So could somebody else."

"That is pure supposition."

"With respect, sir, no—it is a possibility, of which account must be taken in conjunction with certain other circumstances that seem to have been overlooked at the time."

"Those being?" Mr. Chubb's tone had cooled perceptibly.

Purbright prepared to enumerate on his fingers. "One: the regrettable but widely acknowledged fact that Bernadette Croll was ardently promiscuous. Two: that analysis at postmortem showed that she had consumed something on the order of two or three double brandies that evening. Three: that a candle on a stand, seen burning inside the church at about midnight, close to where Mrs. Croll's body was later found, had been removed by the time the police were called and photographs taken. Four . . ."

"Oh, come now, Mr. Purbright. I think I know the source of that one. Someone has been telling you what the little village boy was supposed to have seen. Am I right?" Mr. Chubb's was the magnanimous smile of the about-to-score.

"Sir?"

"Boy with an odd name," said Mr. Chubb. "The illegitimate son of the lady who works in the village pub. Mentally defective, poor little chap. I don't think you need worry overmuch about lights at midnight if it was young master whatsisname who saw them."

"Howell," Purbright said.

The chief constable looked blank.

"Howell—the boy's name is Howell, sir."

"I see. Yes. Anyway, his mother wrote quite a nice little letter apologising for the trouble he'd caused, and that was that as far as we were concerned, although I believe there was some talk of an application to the magistrates for a care and protection order."

"That would be up to the county welfare committee," said Purbright.

"Of course."

"The chairman of which is Councillor Robin Cork-Bradden."

After a pause, the chief constable said pleasantly: "I'm sure that the relevance of that information is clear to you, Mr. Purbright, but I'm afraid it eludes me."

"I'm sorry, sir; I thought you would know that Mr. Cork-Bradden lives at Mumblesby. At Church House, in fact. So the case of Miss Howell and her child is perhaps familiar to him."

"Possibly." Mr. Chubb glanced at his watch, then towards his half-read Flaxborough *Citizen*. The inspector rose, whereupon Mr. Chubb unmoored from the mantelpiece and returned to the table.

He spoke quietly, apparently to the newspaper.

"I realise that Superintendent Larch was not always quite as painstaking as we try to be, but it would be rather a pity, now that he has retired, if that little bit of assistance he gave us last year should prove to have been misdirected. Very upsetting for a chap after so many years in the Force."

"Very," Purbright agreed, before leaving the office.

Half an hour or so later, Mr. Chubb reached the back page of the *Citizen*, in the first column of which it was customary to print the Thanks and Acknowledgements relating to the week's bereavements.

Under "Loughbury" appeared a sizeable recital of gratitude. Its objects included the doctors and nurses of Flaxborough General Hospital, Steven Winge Ward; the Reverend Alan Kiverton; Messrs. K. Bradlaw and Son, for tasteful funeral arrangements; the senders of all the beautiful floral tributes, too numerous to be listed; the Grand Master and Officers of the Tom Walker Lodge, Chalmsbury; several army and professional organisations; the Chief Constable of Flaxborough (Mr. Chubb eyed this item with distinct nervousness); the firm of brewers that owned the Saracen's Head, Flaxborough.

There followed an item that disconcerted Mr. Chubb even more than had the appearance of his own name.

"Special thanks from the Mumblesby Relic Committee to Detective Inspector Purbright for kind services in protecting my late husband's Memorial Presentation to Our Village."

There was no telephone in Mr. Chubb's room, or he might have used it in token of his disquiet. He went instead to the duty sergeant's office and asked him to summon the inspector. Purbright, though, had gone out. Mr. Chubb returned to his room, where he solaced himself until lunchtime with back numbers of *Horse and Hound*.

The chief constable was not the only reader of the *Citizen* that morning to take particular notice of Zoe Loughbury's announcement.

Mrs. Priscilla Cork-Bradden, of Church House, Mumblesby, who had been looking through the paper while seated in a garden chair, was so intrigued that she came indoors at once to her husband.

"What in heaven's name is the Mumblesby Relic Committee?"

Mr. Cork-Bradden put down the fishing fly he had been contriving from pieces of feather and cane. He stared at her dully.

"There's no such thing."

"Darling, it's here in the local rag." She gave the newspaper, already disarranged, a shake. Two sheets fell to the floor. She waited to see if her husband would pick them up, but he was looking at his fly-tying again.

The part of the paper containing the thanks notice was still in Priscilla's grasp. She folded it and flipped it with her fingertips.

"There you are—'Mumblesby Relic Committee.' I'm not stupid, darling."

She read a few more words, then looked up angrily. "My God! 'My late *husband* . . .' *Her* late husband! The paper should vet these things before accepting them from people like that dreadful Zoe or whatever they call her. You're a director, darling: you'll have to have a word with the editor."

"It doesn't have an editor now," said Mr. Cork-Bradden. He sounded a little weary. "If you remember, the board took the opportunity when old Kebble retired, to merge editorial direction with advertising."

Priscilla quoted further, more bitterly. "'My late husband's memorial presentation' . . . What is that supposed to mean?"

Her husband took the paper from her, gently, and read it for himself. He had a long face, with slightly protuberant blue eyes and high cheekbones. His hair, pale and thin, was brushed straight back from the high, narrow forehead.

His movements were few, but in this comparative immobility there was nothing relaxed: he had the posture and air of an invigilator. The mouth was level, the lips thin but well shaped and sensitive. When he spoke, they scarcely moved; yet very rarely was he ever asked to repeat anything he had said.

He returned the paper to his wife.

"Purbright is a police inspector at Flaxborough," he said. "Of what he has to do with Miss Claypole, I have no idea."

Priscilla watched him pick up a pair of tweezers and capture a fragment of bright yellow feather that her brusque arrival had sent looping and gliding to the floor.

She straightened and demanded coldly: "And *our* things? Are policemen protecting *them?*"

He glanced at her, then went on with what he was doing. "It will serve no purpose," he murmured, "to be hysterical about them."

A drawstring of anger tightened the woman's mouth. She spoke slowly and quietly.

"Robin . . . when are we going to get them back?"

He delayed his answer as if to mark his contempt for the question.

"When?" she prompted curtly.

Again a pause. Cork-Bradden finished squeezing a tiny bead of glue to the pared spine of the yellow feather. He applied the feather with loving delicacy to the twine-bound shank of a fishhook. To his wife he said:

"As I have tried to make clear more than once, everything the man extorted will be brought back here in due course. But there are certain precautions to be taken first. I do not wish to sound critical"—and here the note of weariness became more pronounced—"but to continue harping upon an already perfectly well understood situation could begin to sound a little vulgar."

"Vulgar?" Mrs. Cork-Bradden repeated, icily.

"Just the tiniest bit, yes." He twice looped twine to secure the yellow wing of the fly, then peered about the desk top. "You haven't seen my razor blade, have you?"

"I should never have supposed," said his wife, "that a little vulgarity would offend anyone so richly endowed with the common touch as to enjoy screwing the village scrubber."

Mr. Cork-Bradden sorted among the objects near at hand until the blade came to light. He began planing wisps of cane from the fly's body. "It wounds me, my dear, to learn after all this time that it was not sexual displacement but simple snobbery that lay behind your disapproval of poor Bernadette."

CHAPTER 11

Leonard Palgrove scuttled from table to table in the Old Mill Restaurant and satisfied himself that Mrs. Gordon, the help, had set all eighteen places right-handedly and remembered to put plastic protection beneath the table linen on table four, reserved for Mr. Winston Gash's party. He checked the provisioning of the bar, made sure that the front door was unbolted, and hastened to the kitchen.

Mrs. Gordon, a solid, big-boned woman, whose shortsightedness compelled her to squint at the task in hand with an expression of deep anxiety and mistrust, was thawing out frozen scallops in a saucepan: scallops were to be what the menu termed "Off-we-Goes" that evening.

"Make sure they're done enough," commanded Mr. Palgrove in passing. Mrs. Gordon scowled at his back and turned up the gas to blowtorch ferocity. It was turned down again by Cynthia Palgrove, who had just come from the pantry with a tray of frozen steaks.

"Mester says that . . ." Mrs. Gordon began.

"Sod the mester," Mrs. Palgrove advised. She put the tray on the table, made a quick count of the pieces of meat, and departed. Mrs. Gordon smiled to herself and burrowed beneath her pinafore to scratch her armpit.

Mrs. Palgrove made her own table tour. She replaced five forks, two spoons and a knife, and repolished three of the wineglasses.

"Now what's wrong? I've been round once."

Leonard had donned his Jolly Miller set. He now was wearing breeches, white stockings, buckled shoes and a kind of nightcap in red wool.

Instead of a waiter's napkin, there was draped on his arm a sack with FLOUR in big black letters.

"Everything's fine," Cynthia said to him sweetly. She bent to rearrange some of the stuffed sacks on the two millstones that served as seating in the space before the bar.

Mrs. Palgrove was not dressed as the Jolly Miller's wife. She made no personal concessions to the element of uninhibited make-believe that she considered important to a restaurant's profitability. "Fun," in Cynthia's vocabulary, was an adjective, never a noun.

"Who's the unlucky girl that Spence is bringing?" Palgrove inquired.

His wife lifted one shoulder a fraction to indicate indifference. The shoulder had an end-of-summer tan; it was lean but elegant. She wore a dress of such deep cleavage that it resembled a long pair of partly drawn curtains, with a glimpse of navel at the bottom of the V, like the eye of an inquisitive neighbour, peeping out.

"They reckon," said Leonard, "that it's that bint who used to shack up with Rich Dick. She's supposed to be after his place on the Hunt Committee."

"A night with Spence would be a high price."

"One with Winnie would be a bloody sight worse."

Mrs. Palgrove winced. She checked from where she stood that there was on every table a salt hopper and its companion model of a mill that dispensed pepper when its wheel was rotated.

Quietly, she said: "Talking of Rich Dick and his lady friend . . ." and paused, meaningfully, while still eyeing the tables.

"Yes, love?" The Jolly Miller was attentive, obliging, not knowing quite how he might serve.

His wife continued to look away from him, across the room.

"The little painting of Mummy's?"

"Ah, the little milkmaid thing. Sure. Yes, I hadn't forgotten, sweetheart."

"The little Corot," Mrs. Palgrove said, with quiet emphasis. "And you'd better not have forgotten."

The Miller wanted to say, "Christ!" but managed not to. He put out one hand, sighed, tugged at his fun hat. "It was only a loan. I told you. And *she* knows it was a loan. Look, I could hardly barge in and snatch it straight after the bugger's funeral, could I? Don't worry. I'll not forget."

"I was talking to Edgar today."

"Edgar?"

"Harrington. He called to make the booking for tonight. And he mentioned that he's been making an inventory for the Zoe woman."

Palgrove looked suddenly anxious. "You didn't . . ."

"I didn't pump the man, if that's what you're worried about. But you can see what will happen next, can't you?"

He shrugged, sulkily.

"She is going to lose no time in collecting her winnings," said Cynthia. "And in cash."

"Cash?"

A ripple of impatience crossed the woman's face. "She'll put the lot up for sale before anyone gets around to challenging her right to it. God, you're . . ."

"I'll try and have a word with her tonight," Palgrove promised. "But it won't be easy."

"No, it won't," said his wife, without sympathy. She peered into the imitation cottage loaf on the bar counter, then glanced at Leonard's hurt-boy face. "More ice."

His look of wounded resentment deepened. She remained looking at him, speculatively at first, then teasingly, almost fondly.

"Shit," said Mr. Palgrove and hauled her into a rough, greedy embrace.

She let him slide a hand to her bare breast and palpate it for a while before she murmured over his shoulder: "You know, darling, if you weren't such a randy old sod, you wouldn't be in the mess you're in now."

The hand stilled at once. Slowly, he drew back from her.

"Mess? What mess?" His flushed face almost matched his fun hat.

Lightly, she restored the hang of her dress. She smiled.

"Surely you can't imagine that I never guessed the real reason why you half-inched Mummy's picture?"

"I don't know what you're talking about."

"Lawyer Loughbury is what I'm talking about, and well you know it. He frightened poor little Len into giving him a sweetener, having found out that he'd been 'having it off,' as they say, with that woman from the farm."

Palgrove's flush was taking on a blue tinge. "That's a disgusting thing to say!"

"What—that you were having it off? or that you let yourself be conned afterwards?" She smiled again and patted his hand. He snatched it away as if she had burned it.

Cynthia sighed and began looking through the menu lying on the bar top. "Grist for the Mill," it was headed. "I could wish sometimes," she said, "that we'd chosen a gimmick with wider scope. 'Lobster Nellie Dean' does seem to be pushing things a bit."

The first customers to arrive were Mrs. Whybrow and her lodger, accompanied by a man of about sixty with a big bull-like head, covered with matted off-white curls like ill-kept astrakhan. This was Arthur Pritty, farmer and demolition contractor, who lived with his three sons at Long Camberley Grange, somewhere in which was also to be found his wife.

The party was attended by Mr. Palgrove in person. He was very jocular in manner, calling Mrs. Whybrow "dearest lady" and farmer Pritty "squire." He was careful not to call Mr. Bishop anything, but as that person spared him neither look nor remark and made his wishes known only through Mrs. Whybrow, it did not much matter.

Farmer Pritty said he'd start off with oysters, and Palgrove said there weren't any oysters, squire, but would he like scallops, which were much the same, really, and Pritty said he'd have a try if they did the same for him as oysters did, and he made a noise like a snorting horse and rubbed his groin.

Mrs. Whybrow ordered "some of those absolutely de*licious* sort of frilly—no, not frilly, *crunch*y—things I had *last* time—those things with *rai*sins or whatever . . . what?—oh God, *you* know . . ."

"Tell him I want tomato soup, Booboo," commanded Mr. Bishop.

Two cars drew up in the marketplace. A Ford Granada discharged a pair of married couples from Flaxborough, bent on celebrating their double wedding anniversary. From the smaller and shabbier car descended a detective inspector from the same town, celebrating nothing, unless it was having just given a lift to Miss Teatime, for whom he hurried round to open the door.

"We are a little early," Miss Teatime observed, "so I suggest we go along to the Gallery. I told Edgar to

wait for us there." As they set off towards Church
Lane, she cast a side glance at the inspector. "Nice
suit," she murmured.

Purbright took her offered arm. "My sergeant told
me it costs all of eight pounds to eat at the Mill," he explained.

"You will reclaim it on your expense account,
surely?"

"The last sybarite on the Flaxborough force was re-
duced to the ranks for charging a take-away chop
suey."

Mr. Harrington let them in by the side door. He wel-
comed Miss Teatime with well-bred affability. To his
introduction to Purbright he responded politely, if cautiously.

They sat in the little Georgian-styled parlour at the
back of the shop. Harrington produced a decanter of
amontillado and, for Miss Teatime, some cheroots in a
silver box.

"The table," he announced, "is booked for a quarter-
past eight, so we have nearly half an hour." He used
the pouring of the sherry to disguise his appraisal of
Purbright, who pretended not to notice.

"As I told you earlier, Edgar," Miss Teatime began,
"my good friend Mr. Purbright is interested in the
collection of old Mr. Loughbury."

Without taking his eye from the level of wine in the
glass he was filling, Harrington drew a soft intake of
breath through protruding lips and murmured, "Clean,
Lucy; absolutely clean."

"Yes, well, that is nice to know, of course." She
turned to the inspector. "Mr. Harrington has a very
wide Bond Street-based experience."

Purbright said, "Ah," and Miss Teatime added:
"However, as I understand matters, the inspector is not

concerned with anything so straightforward as theft *per se*."

Almost imperceptibly, Mr. Harrington relaxed. He handed them their glasses.

"No, I had not supposed that any of the articles at the Manor House had been stolen"—this, from Purbright—"but the manner of their acquisition does strike me as having been curious in some cases."

Harrington nodded, carefully. "There seems to be a dearth of record certainly. The transactions must have been rather offhand."

"Gifts?" suggested Miss Teatime.

"They must have been," Harrington said. "There are no receipts, no insurance documentation."

"But why?" Purbright was looking at his glass.

"That, you will have to ask the donors."

"I can hardly ask the beneficiary," Purbright observed.

"What about his widow?" Miss Teatime said.

"She is most unlikely to say anything that might cast the genuineness of the gifts into doubt. In any case, I really don't think she knows. Mr. Loughbury was not a gentleman much given to sharing confidences."

"Not even in bed?"

Miss Teatime regarded her manager sharply. "Edgar, you are in Mumblesby, not Knightsbridge." To Purbright she said: "I have never, to the best of my recollection, been in bed with a solicitor, but I should not expect much in the sharing line even there. My guess is that you are right about Zoe. If so, you can only hope that the original owners will tell you."

To Harrington Miss Teatime said: "The inspector is here tonight in expectation of seeing one or two of those generous people in the flesh. We are to act as his guides."

Harrington sipped his sherry ruminatively, set it

down, and drew a folded paper from his inner breast pocket. All his movements were calm yet precise.

Miss Teatime accepted the paper and unfolded it.

"A copy of the inventory of Mr. Loughbury's objets d'art," she explained to Purbright. "Mr. Harrington has very kindly ticked those items which he believes to have been acquired by Mr. Loughbury during the past year or so. He has pencilled against each the initials of the person who owned it previously."

"To the best of my understanding," qualified Harrington.

Purbright glanced down the list. "You've been extremely helpful," he declared.

"Of course," added Miss Teatime, "you have the inspector's assurance, Edgar, that the information will be treated in the strictest confidence. This," and she gave Purbright a Joan of Arc-ish look, "is a private professional document."

"And will be so regarded," said the inspector, "by me."

"There, now," said Miss Teatime, and she leaned forward to allow Mr. Harrington to light her cheroot. His face, as he watched the flame, was as impassive as a butler's.

At the Old Mill Restaurant more customers were arriving. By the time that Purbright and his couriers took their seats at a corner table under the effusive direction of Jolly Miller Palgrove, there were more than a dozen people in the room.

Zoe Loughbury, née Claypole, recognised Miss Teatime at once and waved. Miss Teatime waved back. Purbright bowed, a little shyly. Zoe's frown of uncertainty blossomed suddenly into a smile. She called across. "Hi! Sorry—you look different away from the bathroom."

They saw Zoe's companion, Spencer Gash, give them a long, mistrustful stare before turning to her with a question.

Harrington identified Gash for Purbright's benefit.

"By all appearances," mused Miss Teatime, "not a patron of the arts."

Harrington corrected her. "I have him down as Loughbury's source of a rather nice 1735 salver, seventeen and a half ounces. One of a pair bought at auction by his father in the thirties. Winston doubtless has the other."

"His brother," explained Miss Teatime to Purbright.

Mrs. Palgrove was above them, sinuously solicitous. They hurriedly burrowed into menus. After consultation, Edgar Harrington ordered for all. Cynthia beamed approval and glided away.

A good deal of noise was coming from the direction of the bar.

Through the communicating arch, Purbright caught sight of a very large man with what appeared to be a tattered fan grasped in one hand. He was holding the fan aloft while his companions, two women and a short, jocose man in glasses, bayed encouragement.

Suddenly the women began to squeal and jump aside as the big man brought the fan down and mock-threatened them with it in quick, short thrusts.

Some of the diners stared with chilly censure. To others, the turn, or whatever it was, seemed familiar. They joined in the laughter when the little man in glasses, his scarlet face sweat-spangled and contorted with hilarity, staggered through the arch and announced:

"Look out! Winnie's brought his dinner! He has! He's brought his bloody dinner!"

"Who is that one?" inquired Miss Teatime, awed.

Mr. Harrington shook his head. It was Purbright

who spoke. "Car dealer from Flax. Blossom. Alfred. A noted *bon vivant*."

The Jolly Miller emerged from the bar, overtook Mr. Blossom, stalled by his own merriment, and positioned himself by an empty table, where he proceeded to make the sort of gestures that are supposed to help reverse lorry drivers.

The two ladies of the party made a dash across the room and sat down, giggling and patting their chests. Mr. Blossom collapsed into his chair, then slewed it round to command a view of the finale of Winston Gash's performance.

As the farmer lumbered forward into brighter light, it could be seen that the "fan" was a bundle of dirty white feathers. Within it was a scrap of red, and a diamond point of terrified eye. It was a live chicken.

Gash spotted Miss Teatime and halted, staring at her. From within the great cave of the farmer's hand, the chicken also regarded her.

One of the women called out: "Come on, Win, we're hungry."

Gash winked. Without taking his eyes from Miss Teatime, he hooked the middle finger of his left hand about the chicken's neck and slowly, deftly, knowledgeably, pulled the spinal cord apart. A feather floated languidly to the floor. At the point of the beak, there grew a tiny bead of red.

For several seconds Winston Gash remained standing, his smile fixed upon Miss Teatime and her companions. It was the smile of a man deliberating whether to order trespassers off his land.

Miss Teatime regarded him steadily and without expression. Edgar found a distant bowl of gladioli of absorbing interest. Purbright stared placidly at the fast-glazing eye of the hen.

Cynthia Palgrove appeared at Gash's side. She

smiled cheerfully, squeezed his arm, and at the same time relieved him of the hen's pendant corpse. Mr. Gash tried to kiss her. She slipped out of range. He consoled himself with a parting grab at her buttock, then sat down.

"What's she going to give you for the chicken, Win?"

This from Mr. Pritty, who thereupon looked around for anyone whose eye he could catch and treat to a wink of scabrous confidentiality.

"He's a lad, is Arthur," Mr. Spencer Gash informed Zoe. He topped up her glass with sauternes from a litre bottle, already nearly empty.

She thanked him briskly, swigged some of the wine, and resumed her assault on a plate of vulcanised scallops.

"You must get lonely in a bloody great barn like the Manor," observed Mr. Gash. "And cold at night, I should reckon."

Zoe took time off chewing in order to clear a tooth with her tongue. Then a quick shake of the head. "Electric blanket." Knife and fork went back into action.

Purbright tried to make something of such snatches of conversation as came his way. At first he found difficulty in isolating other voices from that of Mrs. Whybrow, but his perseverance eventually demoted it to a sort of carrier wave, omnipresent yet permeable.

"Who," he asked Harrington, "is the gentleman sitting two tables away on my left? Next to the one who called out a little while ago."

"That is Mr. Raymond Bishop. The big man is a farmer called Pritty. Mrs. Whybrow is the name of the lady. She is a widow and rumoured to be well off."

"Mrs. Whybrow *is* well off," asserted Miss Teatime. "She is the former concubine of the wealthy Mr.

Bishop, and she amuses herself by pretending to be his landlady."

"'Former,' you said. Do you mean she's lost the job?"

Miss Teatime considered. "Should we not say, perhaps, that the job has changed its nature. Mrs. Whybrow is now better described as Mr. Bishop's business manager."

"I notice from your list," said Purbright, "that Mr. Bishop made several contributions to the art collection at the Manor House. One, if I remember, was that quite splendid punch bowl in the sitting room on the first floor."

Miss Teatime's soup spoon paused on its ascent. "You seem to have enjoyed a more extensive tour of the house than we have, Inspector."

"Purely fortuitously. Fire was rumoured. I happened to be near at hand."

The well-bred Mr. Harrington concealed his scepticism behind his napkin.

Reaction from Miss Teatime was more direct. "Ah, hence the intriguing announcement in this week's local newspaper."

The inspector looked blank.

"On behalf," said Miss Teatime, "of the Mumblesby Relic Committee."

She waited a moment. The inspector said nothing.

"It seems you saved something or other that had been presented to the village by the late Mr. Loughbury. A relic? I should love to know what it was—or is."

Purbright gave in.

"So should I."

CHAPTER 12

Had Inspector Purbright been paying less attention to what was happening inside the Old Mill Restaurant, he might have noticed the passing of a very unusual vehicle outside.

It was monstrously large. Each of its four wheels was the height of a man and bore a tyre the girth of a beer barrel. The sound as of an ore crusher came from the engine in its long rectangular box, gashed with cooling vents and surmounted by a great mushroom-shaped exhaust.

The cab was set high above the front pair of wheels. It was a steel-ribbed glass tank that in daylight exhibited the driver, arms, legs and all, with a sort of brash candour. Now, at dusk, he could be seen only in silhouette, a high-perched figure lurching and wrestling with levers.

The machine ground ponderously past a row of parked cars, then swung abruptly through ninety degrees and began to cross the empty square towards the Manor House.

There was a broad paved alley on the south side of the Manor House, leading to what once had been stables.

Very slowly, as if the bearing strength of the ground beneath were being assayed, the vehicle moved into the alley like a huge hermit crab annexing a shell.

It was brought to a halt at a point opposite the centre of the gable wall. To the grinding throb of the engine was added a high whine as four stabilising rams descended from the underbelly.

The darkness was thicker in the shelter of the house, and the only witness of what was happening there was a child who saw the machine arrive in the village and had furtively followed it. Now he made the extraordinary discovery that it had a neck.

He watched this neck as it stretched aloft, retracted a little, descended, and bore its head forward almost to the wall of the house. It moved next in slow, exploratory arcs, as if in search of concealed prey.

The neck, in fact, was an articulated boom; the head, a heavy, cuspidal grab.

After a while, the lateral movements of the boom ceased and a gear change drew from the engine a deeper, more powerful surge of sound. The boom swung back all of a piece, joints locked, head rigid.

It was poised in the sky like a great hammer.

The child had ventured, bit by bit, into the alley, but his back and hands were pressed to the wall behind him, spring-loaded for flight.

The note of the engine changed once again. It spoke to him of immediate menace. He crouched low and scuttled back to the corner, where he clung to the wall as to a mother's skirt.

Suddenly, there ran through the stone beneath his hands a heavy shudder, like that of an old horse, pained by a kick.

Moments later, a second shock reached the child. He heard a rumble of falling masonry.

When he peeped again into the alley, the neck was drawing back for another strike. The child sniffed the acrid smell of ancient plaster. A cloud of dust was rolling slowly from the alley into the light of a street-lamp.

He darted through the dust and sheltered against the house on the further side.

From there, the view was better.

A small, but excitingly dangerous-looking hole had appeared in the gable wall about midway between ground and roof apex. A thin, black fissure had been opened, and some stone facing had peeled off.

The machine launched its third strike.

The boy shut his eyes but heard a sound so unexpectedly dull (it reminded him of when he had knocked a melon off the top shelf of his mother's pantry and heard it burst on the stone floor) that he felt cheated and opened them again.

Disappointment changed instantly to horrified admiration.

A section of wall ten feet across was bulging outward. Here and there, a piece broke off and crashed to the ground. Then, quite slowly, the whole great blob split and sloughed away and sank, growling, into a cauldron of dust.

For a long time Oggy Howell stared up at the gaping rooms that were slung so precariously, it seemed to him, in the sky. The shapes within were too shadowy to identify, but he sensed them to be intimate and secret things, which the light of morning would outrageously display.

He waited until the machine had retracted its rams, backed out of the alley, and rumbled off across the marketplace. Then he ran to the side door of the Barleybird, confident that news so momentous justified breach of his mother's often-repeated injunction to stay home when she was doing the evening bar.

Sadie's face darkened with exasperation when she heard Oggy's "Hsst!" at the off-sales hatch. She hurried out into the corridor, snatched at the child's arm and shook him.

Oggy was not to be quelled.

"Mam, there was this great big machine, like from Mars, and it had a neck and a great big head, and there was a man in it, and it's knocked a house down in the square there, next to Roger Hinley's house, and this great big machine just went Gthwurrhh . . . and Crump! and just bashed this whopping great hole in the wall and you can see the bed and a sort of wardrobe thing and . . ."

She shook him into momentary silence.

"Austin, if you don't go straight home this minute and get into bed . . ."

"But Mam, it's right what I'm telling you. It did, it knocked the wall down and there was a lot of smoke and that, and there's this great big hole—you can SEE it, Mam—you go and look . . ."

Again she shook him, but with care not to hurt.

"Get off home," she commanded.

"But Mam . . ."

This time she clipped the back of his head. He winced, covered the spot with his hand. She spoke fiercely, pulling him close and bending to him. "If you don't stop playing me up like this, do you know what'll happen? Do you? Mr. Cork-Bradden'll have them take you away."

"Don't care."

She stared at him, near to tears. Someone came into the corridor from the bar. "Hey, girl, we're dying of thirst!"

The man noticed the child. He became solicitous.

"Oh, he's got some cock-and-bull story about a house getting knocked down," Sadie told him.

"It did, it did, it did!" Oggy was tense and resentful now. "A machine knocked it down. A great big machine." Daringly, "And it was from Mars."

"He wants me to go and look." Sadie sighed at the

ceiling, then gave the man, whom she rather liked, a smile.

The man regarded Oggy with an indulgence tailored to please the mother. "P'raps he'll show me, will he?" Oggy ran to his side. The man winked at Sadie and allowed himself to be towed away through the door.

A quarter of an hour later, the partial demolition of the Manor House's gable end was being described, discussed and speculated upon by every customer in the Barleybird. Someone had called the fire brigade, from whose base a report went automatically to Flaxborough police. The duty sergeant entered it in the book under the heading "Insecure Premises."

In the Old Mill Restaurant Mrs. Whybrow was lacklustredly contemplating her *pêche arctique* (a tinned fruit slice on a slab of ice cream) and telling Mr. Pritty about her girlhood devotion to something called a Knickerbocker Glory. "*That* high and absolutely *packed* with the most fan*tastic* whatevers . . ." Mr. Pritty leered and said he knew what she meant.

At Mr. Winston Gash's table, *pêches flambées* were proving difficult; Palgrove had left on them too much liquor from the tin, and the brandy topping would not ignite, despite Mr. Blossom's repeated application of matches.

The two anniversary couples also were in trouble; their attempts to consume remarkably recalcitrant *crèmes caramels* looked like a game of skill involving forks and wet falsies.

Miss Teatime and Purbright had chosen nothing more challenging than coffee. Mr. Harrington was risking cheese. Zoe, eyed admiringly by Spencer Gash, was still busy with her second portion of the main course, infra-red-electrocuted duck.

"Excuse me, but is the lady from the Manor House here, please?"

All stopped eating. There was something about the sudden materialisation of a fireman in full accoutrement, including thigh boots, axe, and helmet the size of a hip bath, that ravished attention even from the cuisine of the Old Mill.

Fire Officer Budge repeated his question. He was joined by Patrolman Brevitt, who had just arrived in his Panda car. Brevitt spotted Purbright. He saluted in an embarrassed way and looked away. A draught of cold night air had entered through the open door.

Zoe rose to her feet, still holding a forkful of duck. She acknowledged that she was the lady from the Manor House. "Christ! It's not on fire again?"

"No, ma'am," said Fire Officer Budge, "but a bit of it seems to have collapsed."

Miss Teatime frowned and leaned towards Purbright. "What does she mean by 'again'? Has she got poltergeists?"

Leonard and Cynthia Palgrove had arrived in tandem to see what was going on.

Patrolman Brevitt stared at the Jolly Miller as if upon a particularly unsavoury case of transvestism. Cynthia made equally cold appraisal of Patrolman Brevitt. "What seems to be the matter, Officer?" Brevitt pretended not to hear.

Zoe fetched her own coat from the lobby. Spencer Gash was staring into his glass and scratching an ear.

Purbright stepped past him and helped Zoe on with her coat. "I'll come across with you." He turned to Brevitt. "Keep with us; I may want you to use your radio."

The departure of Zoe with her triple escort was watched by Mrs. Whybrow with an expression of wry amusement.

"Gone, have they, Booboo?" inquired Mr. Bishop,

who was busy arranging on the table some cigarette cards he had taken from his pocket.

Mr. Blossom made his joke about not paying bills, and his lady companion laughed so much that she spilled some wine.

Winston Gash called to his brother: "You'll not git yer leg ovver now, Spen—not tonight, you'll not!" This so amused both lady companions that they had to grope their way, red-faced and whooping, to the door marked YE OLDE MILL STREAM (*Ladies*).

Farmer Pritty added his mite of consolation. "I reckon 's that other bugger'll be seeing to 'er tonight, me old mate."

Mr. Raymond Bishop smiled knowingly at one of his "Cries of London" and said: "They sound quite happy tonight, Booboo, don't they?"

Mrs. Whybrow was not listening. She beckoned the Jolly Miller to the table and asked him, in gravel-voiced confidentiality, who the gentleman was who had just gone out with that whatsername woman.

A policeman, whispered Mr. Palgrove. An inspector from Flaxborough. Quite a decent fellow, actually.

"Good God," Mrs. Whybrow growled softly, half to herself, "not an*other* one."

At her side, seemingly preoccupied with his ciga-rette-card collection, Mr. Bishop stroked his long nose. Farmer Pritty slumped lower in his chair and flicked fragments of cheese at an empty bottle.

Purbright reentered the restaurant half an hour later. He saw that Spencer had left, as had Mrs. Whybrow, Mr. Bishop and Arthur Pritty. Winston and his party were still there. Mr. Blossom, who wished to enliven the evening with what he called his "squirty joke," was trying vociferously but without success to order cham-pagne. Winston sat drinking whiskies with a steadfast and manifestly lustful regard of Miss Teatime. The lady companions were much wound down and were talking between themselves about electric cookers.

The inspector apologised to Miss Teatime for his absence. He described briefly what had happened

"No one seems actually to have seen anything. A couple of people living nearby heard a machine go by— a bulldozer, perhaps, something of that kind."

Miss Teatime looked puzzled. "You mean the vibration could have caused the wall to collapse?" Harrington said he would have supposed the house to be a notably solid one.

"We shall know more tomorrow," Purbright said. He added, more quietly: "I'm having a man keep an eye on things over there until morning."

"That is very wise," said Miss Teatime soberly. "Tell me, though, is she all right?"

"Mrs. Loughbury? Oh, yes, I think so."

"Upset, though."

"Naturally. There's a fearful mess."

"I shall call to see if there is anything I may do before returning to Flaxborough."

Purbright nodded. "I think she'd appreciate that. Incidentally"—he half-turned to include Harrington—"I do hope you'll have no need to amend that inventory of yours."

Miss Teatime smiled. "Oh, come now, Mr. Purbright —a burglar with a bulldozer?"

He shrugged. "Funny village, Mumblesby."

"A singularly venereal one," Miss Teatime murmured tightly, having sent an inadvertent glance into the furnace of Mr. Gash's stare.

"Do you suspect theft, Inspector?" Harrington inquired.

Purbright had taken note of Winston's interest; he moved his chair to block it. "Walls," he said to Harrington, "do not as a rule fall down by accident when there are valuable things on the other side of them. There is one consolation—a bulldozer is less easy to get rid of than a jemmy."

Mr. Harrington murmured, rather mysteriously: "Low loaders?"

The inspector conceded that there were, indeed, such things, oh, yes. He did not mention his already having ordered the interception of any heavy machine carrier seen on the road within a twenty-mile radius of Mumblesby.

Nor did he share the information passed to him by Patrolman Brevitt a few minutes before his return to the restaurant. This was to the effect that Mr. Brevitt had just encountered, almost fatally, a general-purpose mobile digging and demolition machine known as a SuperDelve 48, abandoned without lights on the highway north of the village, and believed to be the property of A. Pritty & Sons, Farmers and Contractors, of Mumblesby.

CHAPTER 13

The Reverend Kiverton was in a mood of higher elation than usual. A christening . . . heavens, they had not had a christening in the village since his very first month, and that had been a poor, halfhearted affair from the Council Houses. Now, though (and Mr. Kiverton acquitted himself of snobbery because the district council had since put its eight houses on the market and had even succeeded in selling one to the sitting tenant), the ceremony was for the firstborn of young Mr. and Mrs. Donald Pagetter, who had pots of money and a nice sense of style, and were related to the Lord Lieutenant of the county.

"There'll be flowers," Mr. Kiverton told his wife, "and silver tokens, and the Moldhams have lent a christening robe that was used for the Duchess of Argyle."

His wife's eyes shone. "Oh, lovely! And are we to have a proper font baptism?"

"Rather. Won't it be a nice change from those awful utility hip-flask affairs?"

And so, on this Saturday morning, instead of joining the small crowd of spectators roped off from the hole in the Manor House wall, the Vicar of Mumblesby set off for the home of his churchwarden, Mr. Cork-Bradden, full of ideas on how best to promote a baptism of quality.

Sightseers at the Manor House were thwarted of a view of interior intimacies by a large tarpaulin draped over the gable end. They had to be content with the spectacle of Sergeant Love in command of the sorting and sifting of rubble.

The work was being done by two constables. They were tunicless and with blue shirtsleeves turned up, but retained their helmets, on Purbright's instructions, in case of further falls of debris. They looked as merry as new arrivals in a penal colony.

"What I want you to look for, Sid," the inspector had said, "is a piece of wood about so big"—he made a span with finger and thumb—"which may, or may not, still be inside a small steel cage. The cage was set in that wall when last I saw it."

Then he had gone off to ask questions of Mr. Pritty, owner of a rogue SuperDelve 48.

The farm run by the Pritty family consisted essentially of one field (a featureless stretch of soil, three quarters of a mile square) and a concrete runway. The purpose of the runway was to accommodate not aeroplanes but agricultural machinery and the plant used in the contracting side of the business.

There were big hangar-like sheds along one side of the runway. Some were filled with sacks of nitrate, for fertilising the field; in another were stacked drums of herbicides and pesticides. Perched on metal stilts set in the concrete were fuel and lubricant tanks.

Several lorries and pickup trucks stood about. They were dwarfed by a new bright-orange combine harvester and something that looked to Purbright like an armoured car with a huge scoop at the front. Called a "Hedge Grouter," it was capable of riving out all unprofitable vegetation, including small trees.

The inspector walked past the machines and the sheds to the square, grey farmhouse at the end of the concrete. An annex in raw red brick had been added

to the house. Purbright knocked at a door marked
"Office" and entered.

A counter divided the room. Leaning against its far
side, their backs to Purbright, were two men. Purbright
recognised the massive, off-white head of farmer Pritty.
The younger man, who turned his head only long
enough to note the fact of Purbright's presence, had
sleepy, wet-looking eyes with pale-yellow lashes, and a
slightly open mouth. His face was the same colour as
the brickwork. This, presumably, was one of the three
sons.

Purbright waited for more than a minute, but received no further acknowledgement. He said "Good
morning" firmly.

The younger man again looked over his shoulder. He
gave a small interrogatory jerk of the head and opened
his mouth a little more.

"I should like to speak to Mr. Pritty," Purbright said.

The young man smiled slowly at the elder and indicated the inspector with a nod.

"Oh, ar?" The farmer did not move.

Purbright was becoming accustomed to Mumblesby's highly developed economy of motion. He
waited. After a while, the old man again addressed no
one in particular.

"What is it you want, then?"

"I am a police officer, and I should like to know how
a machine belonging to you came to be abandoned on
the public highway yesterday evening."

There was a long silence. Very laboriously, farmer
Pritty launched himself from the counter and faced
about.

"Belonging to me?"

"Yes, sir; it is registered in your name."

"Abandoned? What do you mean, abandoned?"

"No one was in charge of the vehicle. It had no

lights. There were no illuminated markers on the road to give warning. Abandoned doesn't seem to me to be an unreasonable description."

Pritty considered at some length. Then, by a tilt of the head and one sleepily raised eyebrow, he conveyed the message: "You'll have to ask *him*."

The inspector addressed Pritty Jr. "You are this gentleman's son, are you, sir?"

The younger man looked with faintly contemptuous amusement at his sire, then at Purbright. "You reckon?"

The old man sniggered.

A small folded paper had appeared in Purbright's hand. He consulted it, looked up and gave the younger man a bland smile.

"Ah, you must be Lawrence. Is that right, sir?" He glanced again at the paper. "Lawrence Edward . . . committing nuisance by maliciously urinating over seats of open sports car, the property . . ."

A sudden gift of speech, very angry. "That was Harry. What the hell have you got there?"

Bewildered, the inspector checked. "I'm terribly sorry, sir. That was, as you say, Henry. Henry Peter, in fact, June 1976 . . . No, here's yours, sir. Unlawful carnal knowledge of a girl of twelve . . ."

"Bernard! It was bloody Bernard! Why don't you get the sodding facts right before you . . ."

The substantial right arm of farmer Pritty swept in an arc to his son's chest, silencing the rest of his complaint.

"That's enough, boy. Vay-hycles is what we're on about. Vay-hycles. Just you stick to bloody vay-hycles and how they get hijacked."

Purbright regarded each in turn. To the son, he said: "So we've established, have we, that you are Lawrence

Edward Pritty, and that you manage the contracting
side of your family business?"

Lawrence gave a grunt of assent. His father nudged
him. Lawrence said: "That one that you're on about—it
went missing last night."

"You mean someone stole it?" Purbright asked.

Lawrence glowered mistrustfully. "Moved it," he
amended. "Took it."

"Hijacked it," supplied Mr. Pritty again, rather as if
he had bought the word somewhere and wanted his
money's worth.

"Tell me, Mr. Pritty, are the controls of this type of
machine easy to master?"

The notion amused Lawrence so much that he failed
to be warned by his father's scowl. He smiled pityingly
at the inspector and said he'd like to see how *he* got on
with one.

Not well at all, the inspector feared. Certainly not
with the expert knowledge displayed by the hijacker—
quite an old hand, it would seem, at demolition work.

"But why the Manor House?"

Purbright was looking fixedly at Lawrence now.

"And why that particular area of the gable wall? On
whose instructions did you do the job, Mr. Pritty?"

Lawrence's anger deepened the terracotta of his
complexion almost to black. The thin, straw-coloured
brows and lashes stood out like scars. Before he could
speak, his father caught hold of his arm.

"That's enough, boy. Don't let your bloody lard out.
Just tell him to piss off. That's all. Just tell him. There's
nothing he can do to you."

Purbright regarded Lawrence sombrely. "With all
due respect to your father, sir, that advice is not to be
recommended. We are not concerned now with such
boyish pranks as attempted rape (ah, I knew I'd get it
right eventually) but with a very serious matter indeed.

As serious, perhaps, as conspiracy to murder."

"I don't know what you're talking about."

"Whose idea was it, sir? A joke—is that what it was supposed to be? Knocking a hole in a lady's bedroom?"

God, this was awful, Purbright reflected. Like a television script. The trouble was that interrogation of someone like Lawrence Pritty was liable to turn into a sort of extension of the person himself.

"Why don't you tell me about it?" he found himself saying, and worse: "If you're frank and helpful now, you could avoid the main charge."

Lawrence's indolence of gaze had changed to shifty bewilderment. He avoided his father's eye.

"Boy!" commanded the old man. "Get off and see to that combine."

The son remained where he was, staring sulkily down at the counter and picking at a spot near the corner of his mouth. Suddenly he looked at Purbright, his head a little on one side.

"Suppose it was, then? A bit of a laugh. What am I supposed to say?"

From Pritty Sr. burst "Christ Almighty! You wet, mitherin' shithouse!" and he bisoned out of the office.

"It may well be," the inspector said to Lawrence, "that your father is about to warn others. They probably will confer in order to put all the blame on you."

"What others?" Wiliness had survived fear.

Recklessly, Purbright tossed in another line of script. "People in a position to shop you—people who would pretend they're too fine and mighty to know you, if it suited them."

Lawrence smouldered silently for a while. Clearly, the inspector had evoked for him a whole Mumblesby Debrett.

He shook his head. "It was supposed to be a joke on

the cow at the Manor. It's not her bloody house anyway."

"You said 'supposed to be'—do you mean that is what you were told?"

"I only know my uncle Spence was going to take her out for some nosh so as she'd be out of the way." A thin smile came and went. "It was to be a surprise for her when she went to bed."

"Mr. Gash is your uncle?"

"Sort of. Relation, anyway."

"Does he have a grudge against Mrs. Loughbury?"

Lawrence shook his head irritably. "I told you. It was for a laugh, that's all."

Purbright appeared to find this reply reasonable enough.

"Must have been difficult," he said conversationally, "to hit the right spot in that light. There wasn't much room to manoeuvre."

Lawrence glanced down at his hands. In the instant before his face set in sulky indifference, there gleamed a smirk of pride.

Purbright left it at that. He told Lawrence lightly about such matters as signing a statement at police headquarters, and holding himself in readiness for further questioning. Lawrence reciprocated with equally light reference to the probable willingness of his family to pay for the damage if the poor cow—by which the inspector would understand he meant Mrs. Loughbury —sent a bill and didn't get any ideas about making a court case of it.

Then, suddenly, he remembered something.

"Here, what was that you said before, though? Something about murdering. Was that supposed to frighten me, or what?"

"I trust not, Mr. Pritty," said Purbright earnestly.

"What were you on about, then?"

Purbright turned on his way to the door. "You really don't know?"

Lawrence stared and swallowed. "Course not."

"Well, that's all right, then," said Purbright cheerfully. He stepped out and shut the door behind him.

The inspector found Love in his enclosure, seated before a kitchen table which his servitors had carried from the house on Zoe's invitation. Selected pieces of debris lay on the ground around him. Purbright told him he looked like an archaeologist.

"We've found a bit of the cage thing," said Love.

He led Purbright to where a chunk of masonry had been set aside on a sheet of newspaper. Pieces of twisted steel gleamed in the dust.

"There's not a lot of wood," said the sergeant. "That ought to make it easier."

Purbright stared blankly at the twenty or thirty bits of timber that were arranged in order of size on the table. He tried to recall what the Fragment of the True Cross had looked like.

"Has Mrs. Loughbury seen these?"

Love shook his head. "Didn't seem interested." He added, more brightly: "She brought us out some coffee."

The inspector picked up the largest specimen. It was spongy with woodworm and full of dust. He threw it away. Most of the other pieces bore signs of having belonged to the framework of the house. There also were some broken lengths of lath.

"Nothing here, Sid. Keep trying."

He went round to the front of the house and rang the bell.

The door was opened by Mrs. Claypole, fluttery and pale, but armed with the protective indignation of the newly arrived mother.

"*I* should think so!" she declared, rather as if Purbright were an errant son-in-law who had been sleeping it off in the garden.

Decorously, he stepped inside.

Mrs. Claypole's face came close. "Have you seen what they've done to my Zoe's lovely home?"

"I have, ma'am. And I can understand her being very upset."

"*Her* being upset? We're *all* upset, Inspector. It's a terrible thing."

Mrs. Claypole was one of those people who detect disparagement in even the sincerest and most eloquently expressed condolences.

Sternly, she shepherded Purbright into the sitting room.

Zoe was telephoning. She smiled at the inspector and waved two fingers. He sat down to wait.

When she had finished the call, she greeted him again, then asked: "Is *your* house insured against being knocked down?"

"Zoe!" exclaimed her mother.

"Not specifically," said Purbright. "Why, was yours?"

Zoe shrugged. "The insurance company doesn't want to think so. But they wouldn't, would they? They just blab on about riots and acts of God."

"She'll not take things seriously," complained Mrs. Claypole.

Zoe drew up her legs into the cushioned recesses of her chair and wrinkled her nose at the inspector.

He sighed. "I think you should, Mrs. Loughbury. I think also that you should try and realise that there are people in this village who seem to regard you as some kind of a danger to them."

"They're terrified they might find themselves riding next to me on one of their bloody hunts, you mean."

"Language," muttered Mrs. Claypole.

"No, I don't mean that," Purbright replied. "Nor that they fear you might be the next president of the Conservative Association."

"Of course it's that," retorted Zoe. "Do you think I don't know? They've looked down their long horsey noses at me from the moment I carried a nightie case up the front steps. If I'd used the tradesmen's entrance, it might have been different."

"But you do want to take a place in the social life of the village, don't you, Mrs. Loughbury? I saw you having dinner last night with Mr. Gash. Doesn't he pull weight with the Foxhounds Association?"

"The only weight he pulls is his own pudding."

Mrs. Claypole stared, tight-lipped.

"My mother," said Zoe to the inspector, "is, as they say, aghast." She turned. "Mum, why don't you go and make a nice pot of tea, there's a love."

Mrs. Claypole, looking hurt, walked to the door.

As soon as she had gone, Zoe swung her feet to the floor and sat erect. The carefree expression had changed.

She said very quietly to Purbright: "I don't particularly enjoy what is going on, you know."

"No, I don't think you do."

"Of course, she's worried silly, poor old bat, so I can't let on, not in front of her."

"Naturally. But, really, Mrs. Loughbury, we mustn't waste any more time. It's too dangerous."

She shrugged, eyes lowered.

"So you'd better throw some questions, then. The nasty ones first. Before she comes back."

"Very well. One: Are you blackmailing somebody?"

Surprise, indignation, but an immediate reply. "No, I'm bloody not!"

"Right. Two: Do you think your husband was a

blackmailer? I'm sorry about the melodramatic term, but there simply isn't a better one."

This time, Zoe's negative was a fraction delayed. Purbright asked if she would like to qualify it.

"I suppose I would, in a way. Not that I think he went about being a secret criminal. Nothing like that. But people did give him presents. Is that usual with solicitors?"

Purbright said he thought that benevolence in that direction was pretty rare. "What," he asked, "do *you* think about those gifts to Mr. Loughbury?"

"The same as I'd think about anything that somebody shoves into your hand for nothing. A favour's wanted—a favour to match."

"In his particular case, a big favour. You've seen a valuation?"

"Sure. Some very pricey artwork's come in. Nice."

"But *why* did it come in, Mrs. Loughbury? Do you know that? Not, I think, in lieu of professional fees."

"Lord, no. I didn't know much about Dick's business —beg pardon, his practice—but when it came to money, it was either cash on the nail or so soon afterwards the sealing wax was still tacky."

The inspector listened. Distant teacup noises attested to Mrs. Claypole's being busy still in the kitchen.

"You are aware, are you, of the identities of the people who gave your husband expensive presents?"

"Oh, yes."

"And they are . . . ?"

Zoe pouted. "You know yourself who they are, Mr. Purbright. Come on, now."

"I know some. Four is my score. What do you make it?"

She nodded agreement and began counting off on her fingers. "The Venerable Raymondo . . ."

"Who?"

"Ray Bishop—the stuck-up old ponce that Ma Why-brow has in tow. That's one. Then the restaurant bloke, him from Flax, Palgrove. Three, Spence Gash, the friendly farmer. And last but not least, the king of the big givers, Squire Cork-whatsisname."

"Cork-Bradden."

"Yep, him."

"Now, here's another nasty question, Mrs. Lough-bury. Was it these four gentlemen you had in mind when you put that highly embarrassing notice in the paper that was supposed to convey the thanks of the so-called Mumblesby Relic Committee?" He saw the beginning of a grin, and added more sternly: "In other words, were you warning these people off by craftily dropping my name into the wretched thing?"

Zoe gazed at Purbright, at first contritely, then with friendly resignation.

"You're not stupid, are you."

The inspector said he appreciated the compliment, which, he felt sure, was of mutual applicability.

"Ta very much," said Zoe.

"Incidentally," said Purbright, "I know who it was that knocked your wall down."

Suddenly solemn again, she waited.

"No one we've mentioned so far," said Purbright. "He's promised to make a statement this afternoon, and I don't doubt he will. He's a joker. Rather a carnal young man. Somebody put him up to it."

"Aren't you going to tell me who?"

"I don't think I should, if you don't mind. Not for the moment."

For the first time, Zoe looked agitated.

"All right, if you can't tell me who, tell me why . . . *Why*, for Christ's sake? Why should some goon want to . . ."

Before she could say more, there came two inter-ruptions. One was the approach of Mrs. Claypole, pushing a tea trolley; the other, a peal on the front-door bell.

They heard the trolley halt outside the room. Mrs. Claypole, mumbling protests, went on to answer the door. There reached them the voice of Sergeant Love. A few moments later, he was in the room. He carried something loosely wrapped in newspaper.

"I'm not promising anything," the inspector said to Zoe, "but this may be the answer to your last question."

CHAPTER 14

Eunice Kiverton heard the firm stride of her husband upon the path and peeped out of the window to see if what she termed his "raise thine eyes" humour were still upon him. It obviously was not. He was scowling at the gravel as though the devil had planted it with weeds overnight.

The door of the vicarage was not slammed exactly, but its closure was unequivocal. What, Eunice asked herself, could possibly have gone wrong?

By the time he entered the room, Alan Kiverton had composed his features into a smile (his "masterful martyrdom" one, reflected his wife). He sat, his legs stretched out before him, and pityingly regarded his shoes.

Without being asked, she poured and handed him a large, sweet sherry.

He thanked her and downed half of it in one. She awaited revelation, knowing it would be something to do with the lovely Pagetter christening.

"Can't understand the man. I really can't." Half the remaining sherry was disposed of.

"What man, dear?"

"Cork-Bradden. Absolutely illogical. I really wonder if he hasn't gone a bit odd."

She waited, not prompting, one eye on his nearly empty glass. An excellent wife, the bishop once had called her.

"It's the baptism," Mr. Kiverton began. "Cork-Bradden has got it into his noddle that we ought to stick to the 'ordinary drill,' as he calls it. He says he thinks the full-scale ceremonial would be 'inappropriate in all the circumstances.'"

"What circumstances?"

The vicar slapped the arm of his chair. "Precisely. I don't know what he's on about. He may be Vicar's Warden, but this is the first time I've had my judgement questioned on matters of ritual."

"What does he object to?"

"He says the village would be upset if it were thought I was going back to Romish practices, and had I worked out how many gallons of holy water it would take to make any sort of decent level in the font."

"I suppose," his wife suggested delicately, "that that *could* be argued to be a realistic point . . ."

"Not the rubbish about Romish practice, though."

"Of course not. One would think the man was a Methodist or something."

An unamused laugh from Mr. Kiverton. "Not a Baptist anyway. Or one of those Jehovah people. They're all for total immersion."

"Oh, God, and with everyone wearing macks . . ."

Eunice took her husband's glass. "The Pagetters," she remarked quietly, "are much more nicely connected than the Cork-Braddens."

Her husband regarded her with kindly concern, touched with surprise. "My dear, you did not suppose that I might allow a churchwarden to abrogate my authority?"

"Don't be silly," she said, and gave him a kiss and a refill of sherry.

"Dear me, no," declared Mr. Kiverton. "Whether or not Cork-Bradden approves, it is all systems go. If you will see some of your good ladies about the flowers, I'll go over now and check on the font."

Which is where Purbright, making a check for very different reasons, encountered him.

They exchanged pleasantries. The vicar's were perhaps brisker, with hand-rubbing accompaniment: he was wondering how long this rather persistent, though otherwise pleasant, policeman would keep him talking. Purbright's were cover for more serious speculation: how far dare he take into his confidence a man who might well, considering the special advantages of his position, be implicated in what by now was very clearly a village conspiracy?

He decided to take a risk (surely they couldn't *all* be in it, for God's sake).

"Do you recall a little conversation we had, Vicar, on the subject of relics?"

Kiverton tossed his head in good-natured derision. "Oh, good gracious, yes. The lump of firewood, eh? Yes, of course I do."

"I rather think"—the inspector displayed the big, new-looking Manila envelope he was carrying—"that this could be it."

The vicar looked blank. Then, suddenly, "Ah, of course—that shocking business at Loughbury's—the connexion's just occurred to me." He pointed. "Don't tell me your chaps were doing all their sifting for *that?*"

Purbright opened the envelope and slid forward into the light a piece of wood three or four inches long. Two faces were relatively plain; a third uneven, as if it had been split away.

The vicar reached out.

"I don't think we ought to handle it," Purbright warned.

Ah, fingerprints, Mr. Kiverton told himself, quite erroneously. He peered reverently at the exhibit and said: "Mmmm . . ."

Purbright knew this signified merely polite interest, not recognition of the nature of a brown stain with its appended fragments, perhaps of hair and skin.

He left the piece of wood displayed on the flap of the envelope.

"I don't want you to read too much into this question, Vicar, but can you call to mind any article in the church—anything commonly kept or used here—from which this piece of wood might have been broken?"

Kiverton looked puzzled. "I don't quite follow. What sort of article?"

"Something a man could lift fairly easily. Does one have wooden lecterns? A small table, perhaps. A stool."

"The only table is in the vestry, but that's quite a heavy fellow. And the lectern's brass. Stools, now . . ." Kiverton gazed about him, whistling soundlessly.

Suddenly, he turned and stared, wide-eyed, at Purbright.

"You're looking for a weapon! A weapon—here in the church!"

Purbright raised a hand. "I am simply examining possibilities, Mr. Kiverton."

The vicar threw a glance to the tower gallery. For an instant he cowered, as if threatened.

"Not that poor woman who . . ."

The man was by now so obviously alarmed that Purbright abandoned diplomacy.

"We no longer believe that Mrs. Croll died as the result of a fall. We think she was attacked and struck down."

"What, *here?* Attacked?"

"Here, yes."

"In a locked church?"

"Churches are capable of being unlocked, Vicar, like any other buildings."

There followed a long pause.

"You must see the terrible implication of what you are saying, Inspector."

"And what is that, sir?"

"Oh, come now. It is obvious enough. If what you say is true, and this appalling thing has been done . . . oh, but no, you cannot be making such an accusation . . ."

"I have accused no one, Mr. Kiverton."

"But the keys, man. The keys. You talk of unlocking. Locking, unlocking—and by whom? A murderer? There are only two keys. Two, that's all. I have one. My warden has the other. Which of us are you going to arrest, Inspector? Or is it to be both of us?"

Purbright had caught a strong whiff of sherry. He gave Mr. Kiverton what he hoped was a reassuring smile.

"It is scarcely likely that I should be talking to you so frankly, sir, if I had any intention of arresting you. As for Mr. Cork-Bradden, I don't doubt that he will be able to give his own account of such matters as I might need to have explained to me."

The vicar looked a little abashed. "This comes as quite a shock, you know, Inspector."

"Of course, sir."

"Especially as we were just preparing for a joyful occasion. Our first baptism in the village for more than a year. We could have done without this . . . this unexpected shadow."

For the next half hour or so, and with the vicar's permission but not his company, Purbright roamed every accessible part of the church on the lookout for potential blunt instruments. Nothing suggested itself. He walked out into the sunshine.

The ancient yew trees in Mumblesby churchyard looked solid and nearly black against the bright sky. When the light was not behind them, though, they had a curious viscous appearance, like hangings of dark-green lava.

Beyond the yews and huddled beneath the tresses of a vast arthritic willow, were some of the oldest graves in the parish. Their headstones leaned at random in the rank grass, peaceful as sleeping drunks.

Purbright strolled idly among the dead, deciphering here and there a name or a date. It was not a profitable, nor even in any sense a relevant, occupation, but it served to delay his call upon one of the living, to whom he was by no means sure what to say.

It was when Purbright had reached the limit of this part of the burial ground and was about to descend to the path leading to Church House, that he happened to glance across to one of the plainly glazed windows of the church.

He stopped and stared, transfixed by the wild impression that the church, like some great stone ship, was slowly sinking, and that this had been brought about by none other than the vicar himself—its captain, as it were—whose hauling upon a rope had opened the sea cocks.

The illusion lasted only a moment. It was not the church that was sinking, but something within it—an object of considerable mass, whose immobility one took for granted—that was just as improbably rising.

The great seventeenth-century font cover of carved oak had parted from its octagonal base, the much more ancient font itself, and was being slowly drawn aloft.

Eventually, Mr. Kiverton stopped pulling and lightly wound a few turns of rope round a cleat in a nearby pillar.

The font cover (it looked, Purbright decided, rather like a junior version of the Albert Memorial) was by now suspended at a height of three or four feet above the stone basin. Plenty of room, he supposed, to manoeuvre a baby into the prescribed baptismal attitudes.

The vicar stepped up to the font and leaned forward to inspect the basin.

Suddenly he frowned and pouted in a good-gracious kind of way. He reached down into the font and picked something up. Whatever it was, it was too small for Purbright to identify from where he stood.

For some moments, Mr. Kiverton examined his find on the palm of his hand. Then he wrapped it in a piece of paper. He was about to put it in his pocket when his eye happened to meet the inquisitive gaze of the inspector.

At once, he held up the discovery and signalled by gesture that Purbright was welcome to share it.

The inspector returned to the church. Mr. Kiverton had not moved.

"In the font," he said. "How awfully odd."

Purbright stared for a full minute at the little silver-cupped jewel that the vicar had handed to him.

When at last he raised his eyes, it was to seek out the arched top of one of the lancet windows. Then his regard moved to the font and, finally, to its suspended cover.

Mr. Kiverton saw Purbright's face muscles tighten, as if with pain, and heard a softly suspired "Christ!"

CHAPTER 15

Ever since his breakfast-time encounter with Zoe Loughbury, Mr. Buxton had found room among his sizeable collection of uncharitable sentiments to include the faint but attractive hope that his late employer had met his end by other than natural causes.

Why otherwise, he asked himself, should the widow be so cheerful and at the same time so insensible of the sanctity of legal protocol? Her attitude towards the late Mr. Loughbury's testamentary disposition ("will," indeed!) had been almost flippant. This was not the behaviour to be expected of a woman bereaved.

"It was almost," Mr. Buxton had told his own, very respectful, wife that evening, "as if she regarded me as somebody from the Pools."

He did not mention Zoe's greater sin: her failure to make the bearer of good tidings the recipient of her personal gratitude, there and then.

That was not the only circumstance that fuelled Mr. Buxton's suspicion, of course. The marriage itself, furtively procured by special licence and largely unacknowledged by the sort of people with whom Mr. Richard normally associated, had run less than a year of its course. (*I put it to you, madam, that you could not wait for the Great Reaper to drop a fortune into your lap: you had to wield the scythe yourself, did you not?* Thus Buxton, the eminent silk, cross-examining in his own head.)

And why, if the death of the senior Partner had been

straightforward, were the Flaxborough police now making inquiries?

He himself had seen an inspector of his acquaintance call at the Manor House, and there was talk among the solicitors about visits to the village by a detective sergeant.

But the best of all Clapper's reasons for sanguinity lay in a locked drawer in the church close offices of Loughbury, Lovelace and Partners.

It was an envelope containing a number of foolscap pages that Loughbury had personally and privately covered with his tight, meticulous lawyer's script nearly twelve months ago—shortly after his marriage, in fact. (*You might well consider that significant, members of the jury.*)

Sealed with the green wax that the Partners reserved for especially confidential items of business, this envelope had been consigned to Buxton's keeping, with the injunction (humorously expressed, he remembered, for Mr. Richard was quite a droll old gentleman) that it be opened only in the event of his dying suddenly.

What was Clapper now to do with it? He could simply pass it on to one of the Partners. Or destroy it unread, for the knowledge of its existence was his alone. He was strongly tempted to open the envelope and judge of its contents himself, but he doubted if he could reseal it convincingly.

For a long while after the Partners, the two ladies who wore woollen jumpers and typed, and Mr. Loughbury's temporary replacement, young and pernicketty Alexander Scorpe, had gone home on that Monday evening, Mr. Buxton sat in the seclusion of his own cubbyhole of an office and gazed at the well-filled packet and wondered if it contained the means of bringing to book the disrespectful widow.

At last, he put it into the case in which Buxton Q.C.

daily carried his imaginary briefs and his real sandwiches. He telephoned police headquarters in Fen Street. Was the chief constable by any chance still upon the premises? Robert Buxton, of Loughbury, Lovelace and Partners. No, the sergeant would *not* do. Yes, he would hold the line.

Mr. Chubb was not at Fen Street. He was in the company of his Yorkshire terriers, geraniums and wife at his home in Queen's Road. But as he knew Mr. Buxton to be a solicitor's clerk and hence likely neither to petition nor to canvass on his own behalf, Mr. Chubb magnanimously suggested that he "call on his way home." (Clapper dwelt in a semidetached villa at the better-but-not-much end of Jubilee Park Gardens, off Queen's Road.)

Entrance to the chief constable's house was through a big conservatory-like porch. All the woodwork was painted white. The outer doors were plainly glazed, the inner ones had frosted panes, bordered by stained-glass segments. Within the porch, four white urns held plants with clusters of pink flowers. Mr. Buxton did not know what they were.

Response to his ring—it was by Mrs. Chubb—was prompt enough, but both sets of doors seemed difficult to open. Her plump, good-natured, motherly face reddened as she pushed, pulled and rattled.

"It's the boys, you know," Mrs. Chubb said, when at last a way into the house had been won. "The dogs. We use the back as a rule. Then there's no problem. Never mind, Father's expecting you."

Mr. Buxton sniffed secretly. There was a distinct smell of kippers. It did not seem right. Common. Dog food, perhaps?

"We've had tea," remarked Mrs. Chubb, cheerily, "so you can go into the lounge."

Which is where the chief constable was already installed, his spare, almost frail figure propped lightly against the wall by the fireplace.

Upon Buxton's entry, Mr. Chubb withdrew his hand from the pocket of the long grey cardigan that was his domestic livery and indicated a chair. He did not exactly greet his visitor, but he looked relaxed and tolerant.

"And what can we do for you, Mr. Buxton?"

The chair was as submissive as quicksand. Clapper's backside sank so deeply and his knees were left so far overhead that his struggle to open his briefcase made him look like an escapologist rehearsing a new trick.

Mr. Chubb waited patiently, then stepped forward to receive the extricated package.

"You say you want me to open this? It is sealed, you know." He turned the envelope about in his hand and looked at it without enthusiasm.

Clapper climbed out of the embraces of his chair and perched himself on its edge.

"It was sealed by Mr. Richard," he said. "I have full responsibility for its custody and disposal, naturally." His original intention to address the chief constable with professional familiarity as "Chubb" seemed now less commendable.

Mr. Chubb laid the package gently on the mantelshelf. "Perhaps," he said, "you had better tell me all about it."

Buxton Q.C. outlined the case for the prosecution. It took considerably less time than he had supposed it would. Mr. Chubb heard him out without interruption.

There followed a silence. Clapper cast a few exploratory glances about the room, hopeful that they might reveal a decanter. He was disappointed.

The chief constable frowned at his fingernails. "There is one strong objection to what you suggest, I'm afraid, Mr. Buxton. Mr. Loughbury was having medical care over a period of weeks; he died in hospital, and the doctors were quite satisfied as to the cause of his death."

Buxton Q.C., thwarted spirits fancier, countered: "My position is simply this, Chief Constable: I should not feel happy if Mr. Richard's confidence in his friends on the police force failed to prevail over a formality such as a medical certificate."

Mr. Chubb tried to work that one out. He asked: "Do you mean that Mr. Loughbury expressly wished his letter to be opened and read on his death, irrespective of circumstances?"

It was a good question, and the silk allowed his junior to answer. "Well—yes and no," said Clapper.

In some distant part of the house, the opening of a door initiated a tumult of barking and scampering, with which a woman's cries competed in vain until the same door slammed.

Soon afterwards, Mrs. Chubb appeared, rosy and out of breath. She beamed at the visitor.

"I expect you'd like a nice cup of tea."

She waited for him to taste it. It was lukewarm and much diluted. "Lovely," said Clapper.

When his wife had departed, the chief constable picked up the envelope, felt it, and tried its weight. There was, he judged, an awful lot of reading matter inside. Dick Loughbury always had been inclined to long-windedness.

"I think, you know," said Mr. Chubb at last, "that my Mr. Purbright is your best bet. He knows the district, you see."

A man who could solemnly imply personal ignorance of a locality of which he had been chief constable for over thirty years was too much even for an eminent silk.

"If that is what you would prefer," murmured Mr. Buxton, looking about him unhappily for somewhere to set down his cup.

CHAPTER 16

Whereas I, Richard Daspard Loughbury, of the Manor House, Mumblesby, solicitor, have reason to believe that my life may be in danger by reason of my knowledge of such facts as shall be set forth in this, my statement following, I hereby declare that the said statement is true to the best of my knowledge and belief.

SIGNED, Richard D. Loughbury

WITNESS to signature only, G. R. Buxton

STATEMENT

For the past six or seven years, I have been the legal representative of Mr. Robin Cork-Bradden, of Church House, Mumblesby. I have acted in the same capacity for other residents of the village, including Mr. Leonard Palgrove, of the Old Mill Restaurant; Mr. Raymond Bishop, of Church Lane, the retired orthopaedic surgeon; and Mr. Spencer Gash, the farmer.

In 1978 I was consulted over a land conveyancing matter by another farmer in the vicinity, Mr. Benjamin Croll. In the course of conversation, Mr. Croll made certain remarks concerning his wife's fidelity which I found offensive and embarrassing. He, however, obviously was accustomed to making such comments on the shortest of acquaintance.

About the end of May 1980, I had occasion once more to visit the farm of Mr. Croll, and once again he sought to turn the conversation to the subject of his wife. In spite of my objections, he succeeded in imparting the information that she was now (in his words) being "knocked off" by Mr. Raymond Bishop and that he expected "all hell" to be raised by Mrs. Constance Whybrow, Mr. Bishop's companion of many years' standing.

Although the subject was by now exceedingly distasteful to me, it became clear from the tactful inquiries I made during the next few weeks that her husband had not exaggerated the scope of Mrs. Croll's activities. At least four persons were involved—all, unhappily, clients of mine. Their names appear in the first paragraph of this statement.

This is how the situation appeared to me in the early summer of 1980.

Croll, though complacent to a degree, regarded his wife as a financial liability and a general nuisance. Bishop was flattered, no doubt, by Mrs. Croll's allowing him certain liberties with her person, but the possibility that his consort might find out must have worried him considerably. Gash was Master of Foxhounds; such a position would require any partner in turpitude to be unfailingly discreet, a quality in which Mrs. Croll was notably deficient. In Palgrove's case, not only his marriage but his livelihood would be put at risk by discovery. As for Cork-Bradden, a county councillor and a magistrate, any open acknowledgement of his intimacy with Mrs. Croll would be disastrous.

I did not personally make the acquaintance of Bernadette Croll until I was introduced to her by Mr. Cork-Bradden at a wine and cheese party organised on behalf of the local Conservative Association. Her attractions, sexually speaking, were undeniable and she was having considerable success in selling raffle tickets. My impression, though, was that Cork-Bradden's main object was to "unload" the woman on to me, in order to placate his wife. On more than one occasion subsequently, I encountered her at the Cork-Braddens in circumstances that strongly suggested an actual liaison.

Spencer Gash was another of her "beaux." It was he who provided the money with which she bought the little green sports car that was to become a somewhat infamous symbol in the locality. Gash boasted that year to a mutual acquaintance that he had "laid" Mrs. Croll eighteen times during Flaxborough Fair Week.

In June there were rumours in the village that Mrs. Cynthia Palgrove, joint owner of the Old Mill Restaurant, had left home following her discovery of Mrs. Croll, in a near-naked condition, on the rear seat of her motorcar, which Mr. Palgrove claimed to have been tuning in the restaurant garage late one night. Leonard Palgrove himself came to me shortly afterwards and confided that although his wife had returned, she was determined that continuation of the marriage, and of the business partnership, should be conditional upon his severing his adulterous association. I drew up a document of undertaking and he signed it.

On Thursday, July 17th, I received a visit at my Flaxborough office which, it seemed to me, might well bring to a head the whole unfortunate business. My caller was Benjamin Croll. His wife, he asserted, was pregnant, and he demanded that proceedings for divorce be instituted immediately. He alleged adultery with all the persons mentioned above. I pointed out at once that the law presumed legitimate paternity so long as a wife resided with her husband, but Croll refused to be advised.

Exercising the utmost discretion, I apprised my other clients of the turn matters had taken. All displayed anxiety and distress. It was agreed that I act as intermediary and attempt to achieve a mutually acceptable accommodation.

Croll proved to be less vindictive in mood once he learned the probable total cost of divorce proceedings. He said he would discontinue in consideration of £200 in cash and his wife's undertaking to have an abortion free of any charge upon himself.

The "consortium," as I henceforth shall call the four interested parties, met thereafter and heard Croll's proposition. I undertook to make personal representation to Mrs. Croll with a view to obtaining her cooperation in her own interests.

(I feel that I owe it to myself to place on record here a suggestion which, though "laughed off" by the person who offered it, deeply shocked me at the time. The remark, made by Spencer Gash, was: "I vote we do the bloody woman in and save ourselves all this trouble.")

Mrs. Croll came to see me at my office on July 29th. I outlined the difficulties in which, however unintentionally, she had placed not only her husband but others. Her answer, unfortunately, was to declare herself delighted with her condition and happy to be divorced whenever it suited her husband.

Reluctantly, I introduced the possibility of financial inducement. At first, Mrs. Croll said she was not to be "bought off," as she termed it, but eventually she agreed to give the matter further thought.

On August 6th we had an interview at the Crolls' farm. Croll himself was not present. She told me that she no longer ruled out the possibility of abortion, but her agreement would be conditional upon payment of £5,000 in cash. For £3,000 more, she would undertake to leave the district.

Doubting if such terms would be acceptable to my clients, I made a further approach to the husband two days later. Harvesting had begun, and our meeting took place in the open air. It did not take long. Croll's price had risen to eight thousand. I realised at once that there now was collusion between husband and wife, and I lost no time in warning the consortium of their unethical behaviour.

On August 18th the Vicar of Mumblesby and his family left for a short holiday in the Lake District. The consequent cancellation of services made it a simpler matter for my clients to confer in the seclusion of the church. On the evening of the following day, Mrs. Whybrow telephoned me at home and asked me to come to their meeting place. I did so, and was told that the consortium had decided to make a final, direct appeal to Mrs. Croll.

The settlement they had in mind was generous, and it would be put to her confidentially, there in the church, away from her husband's influence, late on the evening of Thursday, August 21st.

I agreed to be the intermediary just once more. Mrs. Whybrow said something to the effect that I should not be the loser. This intimation of special reward, I had, of course, to rebut at once. I asked for my instructions. They surprised me considerably. The message I was to take to Mrs. Croll was that Mr. Cork-Bradden would meet her "in the usual place" at half-past eleven the following night. If he had not arrived, she was to wait. One of the church candles would be left burning, but on no account was she to switch on any of the electric lights.

It was the first clear indication to me that Cork-Bradden and Mrs. Croll had been indulging in adulterous relations in a systematic manner. Their choice of venue shocked me particularly, attributable as it was to his privileged position as churchwarden. However, it was my clients' contractual dispositions that concerned me, not their morals.

I accordingly attended upon Mrs. Croll the next morning and gained her promise to keep the appointment.

The remainder of the day I spent at my Flaxborough office. Towards the end of the afternoon, I was surprised to receive a telephone call from Mrs. Cork-Bradden. It was an invitation to drinks at Church House at nine o'clock that evening.

Such an inappropriate function did not appeal to me, but I had no wish to offend the Cork-Braddens, so I presented myself at their house at nine and was admitted by Priscilla.

Drinks were served in the lounge. As I had foreseen, my fellow guests were Raymond Bishop, Mrs. Whybrow, Palgrove and Spencer Gash. Another lady was present but she was not introduced, and I learned only later that she was Mrs. Gash. At ten o'clock we were given some supper, and soon afterwards Mrs. Gash was sent home. Mrs. Cork-Bradden excused herself and retired for the night at eleven.

Her husband took the rest of us to his study on

the first floor and poured more drinks. At about eleven-twenty he got up and switched off the light, saying, if I remember rightly, "Let us see if the lady has turned up." He drew back one of the curtains, near which I was sitting, and I looked out. The candle burning in the church was plain to see. Close beside it was something white and rectangular.

I was still watching the candle flame when Mrs. Whybrow said loudly, "There she is!" I saw movement beyond the light. It was a woman, and she came to where the candle was, but I could not recognise her because her face was turned towards the white rectangle. I supposed it to be a notice of some kind. It absorbed her attention.

I jumped when I heard Cork-Bradden's voice behind me in the darkness. He was standing by the door, and what he said was, "Dick, open the window, there's a good fellow; it's getting a bit stuffy."

It was a perfectly ordinary request to make, yet even as I raised the casement catch, I hesitated. There had been a certain self-consciousness in Cork-Bradden's manner, almost as if the remark had been rehearsed. Everyone else was silent, and this added to my feeling of unease.

I pretended the window was stiff because I wanted an excuse for taking so long. I looked back towards the door. It was just closing. A moment later, I heard another door open and close, not far away.

The obvious explanation was that our host was paying a visit to the lavatory before leaving to keep the appointment in the church. It seemed a good opportunity for me to slip away. I pushed open the window and secured the stay, then moved over to Mrs. Whybrow to tell her my intention.

At that moment we heard a sound that drove other matters from my mind. It was a scream, and I would have sworn that it came from inside the house.

I got to the door as quickly as I could, opened it and stood listening. Everything now was absolutely silent. It was Bishop who spoke first. He said, "Hello, it looks as if she's pushed off." Then Mrs. Whybrow said something about the woman being "too damned impatient." I looked out of the window, across to the church. The light was not there anymore.

When Cork-Bradden came back in the room two or three minutes later, he at once switched on the lamp. They told him about the candle going out. I don't think he was surprised. He was pale and did not look well, but he went round refilling our glasses.

I drank my final brandy as quickly as I decently could and prepared to leave. Cork-Bradden saw me to the front door, where he had the grace to apologise for my having wasted my evening. Nothing more was said by either of us. I walked a little way along the path, then stopped in order to accustom my eyes to outdoor conditions.

It was while I was standing there that an alarming thought entered my head. Had that supper party been deliberately contrived in order to compromise me, to involve me in something I knew nothing about?

The more I considered my clients' failure to keep the appointment with Mrs. Croll, the more unreasonable it seemed. I was now feeling angry that I had been considered capable of being duped, and I determined to learn the truth of the matter.

For a start, I would look inside the church.

As I expected, the south door was unlocked (Cork-Bradden would have left it so for Mrs. Croll to come and go). I let it close gently behind me, then, very carefully, I moved forward, alert for obstacles but resolved to use only if absolutely necessary the small pocket torch I always carry when I am out at night.

The first thing I noticed was a distinct odour of cosmetics above the church smells of damp and mould and candles. I thought it a rather cheap kind of scent, not very pleasant. Soon afterwards, my foot struck some metal object. I stepped over it. It was then that I saw something lying further off, dark and shapeless against the paler stone of the floor, and I knew that I could put off no longer the use of my torch.

One hears many arguments nowadays about the definition of death, but that this poor woman was dead could not be doubted for an instant. Some dreadful blow had twisted and stretched her neck like that of a slaughtered bird.

I do not know if even the little light I allowed myself had been noticed, but as I looked down at the body of Bernadette Croll I heard the sound of a door shutting in the distance.

As luck would have it, in the very instant of extinguishing my torch my eye fell upon a piece of wood caught in strands of the woman's clothing. I freed it and thrust it in my pocket before hastening to the door—not a moment too soon, for already there reached me the sound of footsteps on the path from Church House.

That concludes my statement, so far as personal

evidence is concerned, but I hope that before my good friends the police reopen the case in which they were so cleverly deceived, they will permit me to present them (posthumously, alas) with the solution.

It is now clear to me, after reflecting upon all the facts set out above, that Bernadette Croll did not fall from the tower gallery, as was supposed at the inquest, but was killed with a blow from some heavy wooden article which, if not since destroyed, should be identifiable from the fragment I recovered from the body and kept thereafter in secure but visible custody (in the hope that the murderer might thereby be harrowed into confession).

I believe that the supper party at Church House was staged for the purpose of persuading me that Mrs. Croll was killed at the very moment when my four clients were with me and safely remote from the scene of the crime.

In common parlance, I was to be their alibi, should the police decline to believe the suicide story. Had I not seen Mrs. Croll alive and in the church shortly before half-past eleven? And heard the scream she uttered on being attacked?

I need hardly say how quickly I detected the weakness of the scheme. The woman in the church had kept her face turned away. She could have been anybody. I now believe that it was, in fact, Mrs. Cynthia Palgrove, impersonating Bernadette Croll. As for the scream—it is obvious enough that Cork-Bradden diverted my attention to the window business in order to slip out unnoticed to an open window in another room and scream out of it himself.

Given these subterfuges, it follows that the

murder could have been committed at any time between Mrs. Croll's departure from home and my encountering her body.

It will be for the police to establish, perhaps by elimination, the identity of the actual murderer. My long experience of the law leaves me in no doubt but that his confederates will, when questioned along lines indicated by this statement, incriminate both him and themselves.

CHAPTER 17

When Inspector Purbright drove into Home Farm, he found the approach road to be an almost exact replica of the entrance to Mr. Pritty's property. An identical concrete runway was bordered by the same open sheds, sheltering stacks of the same blue-and-yellow plastic bags of fertiliser, the same brands of insecticide and herbicide in their enigmatically coded cannisters. What machines there were, though, looked older, more ill-used, than Pritty's. Purbright identified two spray tenders and a crawler tractor, thickly encrusted with mud. From behind the tractor, Benjamin Croll emerged, carrying two five-gallon cans.

When he saw Purbright's car he stood still stockily, not setting down the cans, and stared. Purbright braked and got out. "Mr. Croll?"

The farmer did not deny it. Purbright showed him a card and told him his name and rank. Croll betrayed no excitement. He was a dark-faced man with a tiny sucked-in mouth. From the exact centre of the mouth hung a pipe. The inspector found himself looking at the ring of whitish deposit, rather like lime scale, that had been formed round the black vulcanite mouthpiece by the constant pursing and relaxing of the man's lips.

"I want to talk about religion, Mr. Croll," said Purbright pleasantly. "Is there somewhere more comfortable we might go?"

Croll's expression did not alter. He seemed in no hurry to be relieved of his double burden. On the contrary, when at last he raised one hand to remove the pipe from his mouth as a prelude to speech, the can was elevated with it, borne on a single finger as effortlessly as a teacup.

Croll held the pipe, stem down, and watched it exude a black, tarry tear very, very slowly.

"What did you say your name was?"

Purbright gazed past him at the charred furrows that stretched into the far distance like a vast oven floor. Croll, like most of the farmers round about, no longer baled and stacked his straw after harvest but took the simpler, if more noxious, course of setting fire to it.

"I've been looking at the statements of witnesses at the inquest on your wife, sir. They contain one or two errors—misunderstandings, no doubt, but it would be better if they could be cleared up." He added, quietly: "I'm sorry if this is reopening old wounds."

Pensively, Croll spat. "I said nowt but what the lawyer told me to say." He put his pipe back in his mouth and moved away. Purbright followed at a companionable distance,

Croll slung the two cans into the back of a pickup truck. He trudged round towards the front, stopping twice to look at his boots and kick one against the other to loosen lumps of clay.

When he reached the driver's door, he found the inspector already leaning against it, looking thoughtful.

The farmer jerked his head. "Come on, shift yer arse or the bloody wind'll change." There was, seemingly, a further acreage of straw and stubble to be burned off.

Purbright stayed put. "Mr. Croll," he said, "you look to be a very busy man. I may not look it, but I am busy also. Suppose we agree to deal in a businesslike way with two perfectly simple questions? Then you may set fire to the whole county so far as I am concerned."

Croll had begun to scowl more darkly, but he made

no attempt to push past the inspector. The pipe was removed again.

"Religion? What d'you mean, religion?"

"No, sir; what do *you* mean by religion? In particular, what did you mean by it twelve months ago when you told the coroner that your wife was religious?"

"Eh?" said Mr. Croll.

Purbright waited placidly. He watched a great blue-grey cloud that was rolling up out of the east. A neighbouring farmer had begun his straw burning.

"No wife o' mine, that'n wasn't," declared Mr. Croll.

Purbright affected surprise. "Oh? She sounded from your own account of her to be a very devout lady."

"Very what?"

"Devout. Caring a lot for God."

"All Detty cared about," averred Mr. Croll, "was dick."

The inspector did his best to sound stern. "Then, why did you tell the coroner that Mrs. Croll was religious?"

Croll regarded Purbright reproachfully. "Are you saying now 's I ought've spoke ill of the dead?"

"You didn't need to make things up, Mr. Croll."

"I did 's the lawyer said, that's all."

"By 'lawyer,' I take it you mean Mr. Loughbury?"

"Ar."

"Why did you think Mr. Loughbury wanted you to say that your wife was in the habit of staying out at night in order to pray?"

The smoke cloud from the adjoining farm was now overhead, darkening the sky. Black motes drifted down. The air had become blue and strongly acrid. Croll's eyes were half closed, and the scowl more intense in consequence.

"Best f'r everybody, mester."

"Not to speak ill of the dead."

"Bloody right."

The inspector nodded, commendingly. "Just one more thing, Mr. Croll." He moved a little away from the truck door. "If you were so considerate of your wife's reputation, why did you tell Mr. Loughbury last July that she was pregnant as the result of her promiscuous behaviour?"

To Purbright's surprise, his question provoked not anger but derision.

"And where," Croll demanded, "did you get hold o' that bloody tale?"

Purbright watched him yank open the door of the pickup, pause, then turn, his face crumpled with genuine bewilderment.

"*Preg*nant? How th'ell could Det be bloody pregnant? We 'ad 'er spayed ten years back 'n' more."

"Do you not think, Mr. Purbright, that this man Croll was lying? From what you tell me, he would seem to be as unsavoury as some of the expressions he uses."

Mr. Chubb had had a heavy day. It began with the discovery that his detective inspector was determined to apply for a warrant with quite appalling implications. The rest had followed inescapably: the rereading of the Croll inquest depositions; a study of the wordy and painfully self-congratulatory testament of the late Richard Loughbury; then a hearing, during the warmest part of an afternoon rendered mortiferous by countless straw fires upwind, of Purbright's account of his own researches at Mumblesby.

"No, sir; he was not lying. The postmortem report bears out what he said."

"Then Loughbury must have been."

The chief constable's tone was uncharacteristically crisp, almost snappy. This straight-to-the-point-ness had been coming on all day. It signified that Mr. Chubb no longer expected to escape involvement in the case of what he rather unfairly persisted in calling "that village of yours, Mr. Purbright." His only hope now was that the more masterful he managed to appear, the sooner it would all be over.

The inspector sensed the new dynamism, and prepared to get the best out of it while it lasted.

"You are right, of course, sir. He *was* lying. In that particular respect, and in many others. Loughbury's entire statement is punctuated with lies."

Mr. Chubb tutted.

"You will have noticed, though," Purbright went on, "that they are not lies of convenience—lies along the way, as it were. They are introduced constructively into the narrative, side by side with established facts, and they seem to build up to a genuine set of circumstances."

He indicated places in the solicitor's statement.

"By the time one has read all these apparently ingenuous references to Mrs. Croll's pregnancy and to her husband's wish to divorce her, one tends to regard both as facts that were never in dispute. But both were myths, myths invented by Loughbury in order to frighten clients from whom he and Bernadette hoped to extort money."

"He and Bernadette . . ."

The words were repeated absolutely flatly by Mr. Chubb. He wanted an explanation, but not at the cost of betraying his own failure to grasp what Purbright was driving at.

The inspector glanced at him admiringly. "The two of them, you say, sir? Oh, yes, I agree. There had to be collusion there for Loughbury's scheme to work. I expect he promised her a share."

The chief constable nodded wisely.

"I wonder," said Purbright, "if ever it crossed Loughbury's mind that he could be pushing his clients too far. I don't suppose he can have envisaged the possibility that the poor woman might get murdered."

The chief constable said he was sure that, whatever faults Dick Loughbury might have had, he would not have condoned violence.

"No, sir, not condoned. Exploited, though, would you allow? Once the murder *had* taken place, Mr. Loughbury seems very promptly to have seen how he might thrive by it."

"You mean these so-called gifts he is supposed to have solicited. He was spreading his net rather wide, was he not?"

"Oddly enough," said Purbright, "I don't think that Loughbury, for all his shrewdness, ever did find out who it was that actually killed Mrs. Croll. But all he needed for purposes of extortion was the short list of suspects represented by those who attended that extraordinary supper party. All felt compromised, and none dare shop another for fear of general exposure. To what extent they had actively conspired to do away with the woman, I doubt if we shall ever know. The person we propose to charge is most unlikely to help us there."

Mr. Chubb pursed his lips and contemplated the cuff of the white linen jacket he had donned in token of hot-weather devotion to duty.

"Bad business, Mr. Purbright, whichever way you look at it."

The inspector, who was perfectly well aware that Mr. Chubb's and his own "way of looking at it" sprang from very different considerations, chose to be perverse.

"Oh, a beastly business, sir, I agree. I don't remember a more impressive mixture of hypocrisy and brutishness."

There was a distinct pause.

"Nor," added the inspector, "a victim for whom I felt more sympathy."

When the chief constable spoke again, it was after he had taken a seat at his desk and spread before him a number of photographs.

"You'll have to help interpret these for me, Mr. Purbright, if you wouldn't mind."

The sitting down was abdication, after a fashion. Purbright resolved not to be too hard on him. He indicated two of the prints.

"This shows the font cover in its normal position; in this one, it has been hauled up on its cable until the rim is at head level, more or less. Once the free end of the cable is secured there, at the pillar—you see, sir?— you have in effect a long pendulum, with the font cover as its extremely heavy bob."

"Weighing what, would you say?"

"Between two and three hundredweight, I understand, sir."

The chief constable turned his attention to a photograph showing much enlarged areas of the cover.

Purbright pointed out some slight irregularities of grain at the rim.

"That is where impact split away the piece that Loughbury found on the body. You can see where the placed has been repaired afterwards, but with a very soft, light wood—probably a modelling wood. It would pass notice in the ordinary way."

The fourth print had been marked with an arrow in white paint. It pointed to a little black circle.

"That is a hole drilled in the opposite side of the font cover," Purbright explained. "A hook would have been screwed in there and a line attached, something relatively fine but strong enough to take the strain of holding that cover twenty or thirty feet out of perpendicular.

"The line would first have been passed through the hole made for it in the lancet window, and its other end made fast in some room on the first floor of Church House. All one had to do then was to wind the line in—by an improvised winch of some kind—and the cover would be drawn over, close to the wall."

"Ready to swing back." The chief constable demonstrated with a pencil held loosely at its end.

"Yes, sir."

Mr. Chubb nodded. "Almost like a pendulum, in fact."

Purbright said nothing.

The chief constable turned his attention to a marked plan of the church floor.

"I doubt if we need puzzle very long over this chap." He pointed to a sketch of the wrought-iron stand with its lighted candle and notice. "It quite obviously was intended to lure the victim into the exact, er . . ."

"Trajectory?"

"As you say—trajectory. There is no chance, I suppose, of finding any trace of that notice so late in the day?"

"No, sir. I think we may assume that it was removed and destroyed before morning during the general arrangements to suggest suicide. The font cover would have been replaced, of course, and perhaps the position of the body adjusted. At the same time, the handbag would have to be taken up to the tower gallery."

Mr. Chubb silently contemplated the assorted fruits of his officers' labours. With his pencil point, he lifted and let fall one of the transparent envelopes assembled neatly on the desk. It contained the earring that had fallen into the font basin. In another envelope was the piece of wood found by Sergeant Love's recovery team, now itemised as "fragment of font cover (ref. print

C).". A third packet was labelled "glass fragments from site below lancet window 2, south aisle"; and into a fourth had been coiled a few inches of top-weight Piskalon fishing line discovered after long and painstaking search in some undergrowth between St. Dennis's and Church House.

"I suppose," said Mr. Chubb, at last, "that hopes of our having been mistaken are by now extremely thin."

The inspector raised his brows in quizzical helpfulness.

"Hopes entertained by whom, sir?"

The chief constable sighed. "I should be the last—as you well know, Mr. Purbright—to discourage tenacious pursuit and prosecution of a criminal, whatever his social standing."

Purbright said he had never doubted it.

"That said," went on Mr. Chubb, "there are features of this present case which I find unfortunate, even if they do not necessarily come under the head of extenuating circumstances. For one thing, it has to be said that the people concerned were terribly badly served by their solicitor. I really cannot imagine what the Law Society were doing to allow him to practise. And then there is the question of the poor woman's own moral culpability. Wouldn't you say so?"

"I'm sorry, sir; I don't quite understand."

Mr. Chubb consulted his finger ends. "Not exactly provocation, perhaps, but what about contributory negligence?" He looked up. "In quite high degree, I should have thought."

The inspector sat on, impassively.

"That scream," said the chief constable, giving no sign of having changed the subject, "was something that Loughbury did not explain."

"No, sir, but by saying he thought it came from inside the house he implied that it was part of the deception—he suggested, if you remember, that someone was impersonating Mrs. Croll at the time."

"Do you believe that there was deception?"

Purbright shook his head. "There was no need. I think the reason for requiring Loughbury to be there was twofold: to compromise him, and to make him witness to a sort of joint alibi—as he himself guessed. What no one could foresee was his taking a notion to go into the church. From that moment, he held an even better instrument of blackmail than the pretended divorce threat."

The chief constable rose from his desk and walked slowly to his habitual position beside the fireplace. He looked thoughtful.

"That scream . . ."

"Yes, sir?"

"You think it was genuine, do you, and not some kind of ruse?"

"I am convinced that it was a real noise."

Mr. Chubb looked pleased to hear it.

"In that case, Mr. Purbright, I hate to have to tell you that your theory concerning the woman's death cannot be sustained. Defence counsel would make very short work of it, I'm afraid."

Purbright appeared concerned. He asked the chief constable to elaborate.

Mr. Chubb regarded first the ceiling, then the view through the window.

"You surprise me, Mr. Purbright," he said. "I am no detective, but I should have thought the objection was obvious straightaway. The woman was struck on the back of the head. So she must have been facing in the opposite direction when this font cover thing swung down. She could not have seen it. People do not scream when there is nothing to scream *at*."

"People don't, sir, no." Purbright began to sort into order the papers and exhibits on the desk. "But I did not ascribe the noise Loughbury heard to a person—certainly not to Mrs. Croll."

"All right. Who *did* scream, then?"

"That word"—the inspector checked that the series of photographs was complete—"was used by Loughbury. He had just opened the window. Sounds carry well on the night air, particularly high-pitched sounds. Soon afterwards, he came across a corpse. He associated one with the other—the body and the noise. Had Loughbury been a detective and not a lawyer, perhaps he would not have made the elementary error of asking *who* screamed, instead of *what*."

Mr. Chubb was paying heavily for a moment of delusively relished triumph. He shook his head, crossly.

"You are not making yourself very clear," he said. "And it *is* rather late. Very well, then: *What* screamed? if that is how you prefer the question to be framed."

Purbright smiled gently.

"The reel, sir. The improvised winch. I do not myself have any enthusiasm for fishing, but even I have heard talk of a reel 'screaming' when the line runs out unchecked."

There was a long pause.

"Yes," said the chief constable. A moment later, rather quietly: "Yes—yes, it does."

Purbright continued to collect together the documents and prints and to check them against a list on the cover of their folder. He spoke without taking his eyes from the task.

"The noise Loughbury heard came very shortly after his host had slipped from one room to another. I have no doubt that he went to watch for the opportune moment for releasing the catch on the reel. It would not necessarily be fixed to a rod; it could have been clamped or screwed to anything stable—the windowsill, for instance."

"At what time," asked the chief constable, gloomily, "do you propose making the arrest?"

"That rather depends on what I hope to learn shortly from Sergeant Love. He's gone over to Mumblesby to make tactful reconnaissance."

"Reconnaissance?"

"They do entertain quite a lot, I understand, sir. One would wish to avoid a clash of engagements, so to speak."

The inspector closed his folder. "I have arranged for either Mrs. Framlington or Mr. Snell to hear the remand application at whatever time the special court can be convened tomorrow."

"The earlier the better," said Mr. Chubb, with what remained of his day's store of decisiveness. "Remand centres are as difficult as hotels these days."

"The prisoner," suggested Purbright, "could stay here in our cells overnight, sir."

For a moment, the chief constable seemed to be having difficulty with his hearing. Then, quite snappily, he said: "Out of the question."

"I'm sorry, sir, but we might have no choice in the matter."

There was a knock on the door.

The chief constable glanced with indifference at the door and again addressed Purbright. "It would be neither seemly nor . . ."

While he searched, frowning, for the word he wanted, the knock was repeated. Mr. Chubb indicated with a peevish jerk of the head that the inspector should deal with the interruption.

Purbright opened the door. He leaned out to lend an ear to brief, urgent murmuring. It was Love whom he ushered into the room.

"I think you should hear what the sergeant has to say, sir."

Love responded to the chief constable's chilly acknowledgement with a boyish geniality of visage emphasised by the wait-until-you-hear-this set of his mouth. Without preamble, he addressed Mr. Chubb.

"Well, as I said to the inspector, sir, it looks very much as if the party's taken off."

The announcement was made so cheerfully that for some seconds the chief constable supposed that this pink-faced young man's irruption into his office had been brought about by some ridiculous misunderstanding.

"Party?" he muttered.

"The party with the double-barrelled name. The suspect." Love now was looking surprised as well as cheerful. He looked from one to the other. "Mr. Cork-Bradden."

Purbright explained for Mr. Chubb's benefit. "It appears that he has left home, sir. Ostensibly for a fishing holiday."

"Where did you obtain this information, Sergeant?" asked Mr. Chubb.

"Oh, it's right," affirmed Love. "The vicar told me. He'd been talking to Cork-Bradden about some christening or other—he's a whatsit, a churchwarden—and according to what was said, Mr. Cork-Bradden must have gone off by car yesterday morning."

Purbright turned to the chief constable.

"It would seem that Mr. Kiverton has been less discreet than we hoped, sir. Of course, he would only need to mention his finding that earring . . ."

The chief constable gently stroked the line of his jaw. "Quite so. And now, as one might say, the bird has flown."

It was a solemn celebration of the obvious. Mr. Chubb waited a moment, as for an Amen. Then he said:

"But you really must not reproach yourself, Mr. Purbright."

of mourners includes an envoy of the Magistrates' Association and also our indefatigable friend, Mr. Scorpe, as ever representing the Law Society. But of the constabulary, there is no mention. Now, I wonder why."

The Rev. Perry paid tribute to the military career of the deceased and to his subsequent achievements in the fields of commercial endeavour and public administration. "His sword did not sleep in his hand," declared Mr. Perry, "nor did he cease from mental strife." Perhaps his interest in the maintenance of law and order and in the moral problems of the young people of today would be longest remembered; but to sport, too, he had made notable contributions, being as keen a practitioner with rod and line as he was in pursuit of Reynard. "It speaks volumes for the wholeness of this man," Mr. Perry added, "that Robin also found time to cherish works of art, with a modest but choice collection of which his own home was embellished."

Zoe Loughbury, her attention concentrated upon the printed page, bit unguardedly upon a coffee éclair. Whipped cream blipped past her left ear. She retrieved it from the shoulder of her dress with one finger, which she then licked. When she had finished reading the account of the funeral, she put the paper aside, stretched out both legs, then drew up one knee and cradled it in interlaced fingers. She stared, pouting, at "Staircase with Valves," which she had lately moved to the wall above the fireplace.

Mrs. Claypole, seated on the far side of the room, prim as a museum attendant, had watched every movement. "You ought to get rid of that thing," she said.

"Why?"

"Because it's awful. I could draw better myself. I can't understand why your hubby gave it house room."

"It was to oblige a friend."

"It would oblige me if you gave it straight back."

CHAPTER 18

A congregation widely representative of public life attended the funeral service in Mumblesby Parish Church yesterday (Thursday) for the late Major Robin Hugh Lestrange Bradden Cork-Bradden, whose tragic death in a boating accident off the Cornish coast was reported in our last week's issue.

The body had been brought back to the village for interment following the inquest at Newquay, at which an open verdict was recorded. The coroner said there was no evidence to explain how Major Cork-Bradden, an experienced sea angler, came to fall from the boat in which he had sailed from Penzance for a solitary fishing trip.

The Vicar of Mumblesby, the Rev. A. Kiverton, M.A., officiated at the ceremony, and a brief address was given by the Rev. Kenneth D. Perry, B.Sc., a "padre" of the Brigade of Guards.

"You were in the Guards, were you not, Edgar?" remarked Miss Teatime. "They actually sent a clergyman along to your squire's obsequies, according to this. How considerate."

Mr. Harrington looked up from his examination of a china poodle. The watchmaker's glass screwed into one eye gave his mouth a slightly idiotic cast. "The army of today's all right," he said. Miss Teatime laughed delightedly.

A little later, she lowered the Flaxborough *Citizen* and frowned.

"Here is a curious circumstance," she said. "The list

Zoe transferred her gaze from the picture to the window, through which some scaffolding could be seen. She smiled.

"If you must know, Mr. Harrington's sending it down for auction at Christie's next month."

Mrs. Claypole's air of disapproval thawed perceptibly. "Oh, he thinks it's worth something, then?"

"Enough to buy a decent horse," said Zoe, carelessly. "And some hunting gear."

Her mother stared.

"I wonder sometimes what's got into you, my girl. The sort of people who go hunting aren't like to want you along with them."

Zoe leaned over the side of her chair and fished up a mug half full of cold coffee.

"They're going to have to get used to it, then, aren't they?"

About the Author

Colin Watson is a former journalist who lives in Lincolnshire, England. He is best known for his series of mystery novels set in Flaxborough, a fictional town based on the seaside town of Boston, England. The Flaxborough novels include *Plaster Sinners*, *Coffin Scarcely Used*, and *Just What the Doctor Ordered*. Six of his novels have been dramatized by the BBC. Mr. Watson is also an expert silversmith, and is a member of the famous Detection Club.